Waters Run Wild 2nd Edition

A NOVEL OF THE WEST VIRGINIA COAL MINE WARS

By Andréa Fekete

black crown

AN IMPRINT OF GUEST ROOM PRESS

Copyright © 2018 by Andréa Fekete
Printed in the United States of America.
Black Crown Books.
An imprint of Guest Room Press.
Charleston, West Virginia/25302
Ingram distribution.

First Ed. published by Sweetgum Press. 2010
Warrensburg, MO/64093

To place discounted bulk orders, email
publisher@guestroompress.com

Cover photo: Joe Reynolds
Cover design: Guest Room Press
Library of Congress Control Number 002120654
ISBN 978-0-692-19745-5

1. Fiction, historical. 2. Fiction, literary. 3. Regional fiction,
West Virginia, United States. 1. Andréa Fekete

Praise for Waters Run Wild

"With language of a poet and surety of an experienced storyteller, Fekete steps forth with a beautiful debut novel in the tradition of Lee Smith and James Still. This is a rich and moving novel that reaches beyond its time and place to capture readers' hearts and imaginations. How exciting to have this powerful new voice among us." **Darnell Arnoult**, author of *Sufficient Grace* & *What Travels With Us*

"*Waters* is a smooth ride over rough terrain: mine disasters, union busting, racially motivated violence, hunger and anger and deep-seated grief. Fekete's fiction marks the place where nature and human suffering meet, the voices of coal dust and rain joining with the general chorus of hard-pressed characters to create some of the most memorable mountain music this side of Lee Smith." **Trudy Lewis**, author of *The Empire Rolls* and *The Bones of Garbo*, winner of the Sandstone Prize in Short Fiction

"Andrea Fekete has a gift. Her debut novel reads more like poetry than prose." **James E. Casto**, *Sunday Charleston Gazette-Mail*

"In its lushness, Fekete's prose is sometimes reminiscent of the magical realist writers of Latin America and especially one of the movement's antecedents, literary feminist pioneer María Luisa Bombal. Like Bombal, Fekete transcends plain realism and interweaves the characters' emotions and thoughts with the landscape—eyes can be "gray and blue like a soft quilt, a sky about to cry all over the dirt" while the mountains are both a stabilizing and oppressive presence—enhancing the stark reality of the hills." **Gonzalo Baeza,** *The Observer*

"*Waters Run Wild* is beautifully written. The prose here sings with a poet's careful touch. Though the topics are as blunt as a baseball bat to the skull, the language never suggests such force. In fact, the narrative's nature, a predominantly woman's tale, seems to welcome Fekete's gentle hand." **Ryan Stone,** *American Book Review*

Dedication

To my grandfather Senon Hernandez Ojeda. Thank you for fighting. Thank you for bringing us to this place called Appalachia. I know you guide all of us still. May the Angels and Saints keep you.

Special Thanks

Thank you to my nieces Katie, Taryn, and my nephew, Trace. Endless gratitude: Mom, Dad, my brother Johnny, the Fekete and Ojeda clans, my "bonus" tribe, the Conn family. A special thanks to my teachers, professors, and the members of the Guyandotte Poet's Society. To my late teacher and friend, Irene McKinney: your time in my life was far too brief. I promise not to "gloss over the hard parts."

Waters Run Wild

2nd Edition

Prologue

The Creek

I tumble down the mountainside, slipping through rocks and dripping, rolling over cliffs in the same rhythm as I have these thousands of years. New birch and young oaks stand where their fathers were cut down at the turn of the century. Weeping willows bow low above me while maples stretch high. Along the narrowing path, a canopy of leaves, light and dark greens flip and turn in the wind like ladies' fans. The leaves whisper brush brush when the wind blows. Forest sounds echo for miles. Caw caw, cinch cinch, caw caw, cinch cinch. Distant sounds, warm, alive and sharp, although the creatures are mostly hidden.

Sometimes there are human voices, like the Grandma who comes by with the chestnut-haired little girl. Anna May plays by me while her grandmother plants their winter garden of cabbage and collards on a south side slope.

Once I heard the grandmother say "I reckon we'll be puttin' that chicken in a pot later. It's finally Christmas Day, Anna May!"

On that day and most Christmas Days, I am frozen but still sneak through rocks beneath the ice. Snow hushes me while the stones on the hillside glimmer and shine under thin layers of crystal, icicles glinting in the sunlight. The grandmother's hands do just what her own grandmother's did and her mother's. They ring the chicken's neck. They pull out the feathers. They wash the raw dimpled skin. The words in the little's girl's mouth—nary, yonder, and reckon are her mother's words and her grandmother's.

Snow mutes the hills except for a few birdsongs curling in and out of the silent wood. My surface is like the mirror Anna May brings in summer to look at her curls. I know Anna's face and the face of miners. I know her grandmother's toil. These are the only people who come this far up the mountain.

The miners walk to work and sometimes stop to look a moment or flick a cigarette near me. I can hear their thoughts like God, don't let me die today. I've seen many a miner come out on a tabletop or a blanket—sons, fathers, grandfathers. When slate falls, women wait outside the mine, sometimes singing hymns and prayers. I sing with them.

I spend my days listening. Human songs. Birdsongs. Noise of animals arguing, making love, and playing. But my song underlies all other sounds, even when I am at my quietest. August heat reduces me to a mere thin ribbon. I snake through the forest almost silently, unnoticed but necessary, like a rug under a sleeping dog or the ground under a stealthy hunters' feet. But in spring, I sing loudest. I roar.

Melted March snow fills my belly and April rainstorms, too. I swell. Say hush hush hush hush. In some spots I say bramble blub, bramble blub. Mostly though, it's hushhh.

Flowers blanket my banks; sometimes maroon

roses melt their fragrance for miles down the holler. Honeysuckle rides on the wind strong like a kite. The smell is sweet and succulent like the taste of apples or peaches. Wild onion fills the air saucy and sharp like a blade. Rabbits splash through me and a bear might wander by for a drink, stretching her neck and murmuring to herself. In summer, children come to catch minnows and crawdads; their bare feet and hands tickle. Summer is hardest for miners for they must walk all the way home through the holler in their thick pit-pants and heavy boots, carrying their dinner buckets.

My favorite time in the forest is autumn. I smell it coming before it arrives. In October, the chestnut shells turn brown and drop from the limbs of the chestnut trees. Leaves large and small shaped like a child's glove, crowns or hearts change into rust or apple-color, sun-orange, and crackling brown. They let me carry them down the mountainside and then the forest smells like old leather or an antique carbide lamp, dust on metal or frost on a window—a glorious smell.

I sing all year. In October when the children dress as ghosts, I sing old funeral songs. I sing for the coal miners carried out on tabletops and in blankets. I sing for the wailing women who stood by waiting. I sing for the midwives who sneak into the abandoned cabin to birth colored babies to poor white women. I sing for the white women who cry as they give those colored babies up. I sing for the bastard babies who die in birth and their teenage mothers' who died with them. Those tragedies come to me because I am the only one strong enough, me the creek, to hold them in.

I hold all their secrets. I sing all their songs.

ONE

Jennie

"It began with snow," Mamaw says.

I answer, "What began with snow, Mamaw?"

When she tells stories, I can see the Mamaw I used to know in her green eyes that feather into gray at the center. Mamaw looks down at Anna May and pets her hair.

Anna still sleeps, curled inside a blanket made out of Papaw's old work shirts and pieces of old quilts.

"The big mine accident that year," Mamaw says. "It began with snow. You was born that very day, Jennie, the day of the mine accident. Was such a bad one folks still tell of it. You come in on the worst day ever could be. I was sick, but we had my neighbor Ester from across the alley. She helped us bring you."

I sigh in relief and smile because she remembers some of it right. I nod. "That's right, Mamaw. *Someone* was born that day." She's wrong, though, about some details. I was born in June. It was my sister Anna May born when the accident happened. But I won't correct her.

She goes on, "It was March of 1913. Why then, Lord, I guess it was Anna's birthday, not yours!" Mamaw laughs at herself in that soft way she does. "And you're my biggest girl. You're eighteen now," she says.

I go to her and sit next to her chair, patting her hand. "Yes and Anna May is five now."

"It must've snowed for nigh on two weeks! We had a couple feet of it. Come clear up to the porch." She laughs again. Then, her expression changes. "But that was a real hard time for th' whole camp. It was so cold. Lord, I 'member how cold it was. Wind come through all the cracks of th' house. We was 'bout to run out of our salted pork. Done lost our goat and et up the one cow we had but for our last cow for milkin'. And there was a shortage of everything." Mamaw breathes in deep and smiles down at Anna. "We brung her just fine, we did. When all that snow melted, the creek got swolled up. It flooded down in that mine and killed all them boys. I set and set waiting to hear who was in it and who wasn't. Your Papaw, thank the good Lord, was home when the mine flooded. Them funerals liked to never end. Went on for days." Her face grows steadily longer and her eyes well up.

I just pet her hand.

"Women couldn't feed their children without scrip to spend at the company store, and they couldn't get no scrip without no men in the mines so. . . ." She sighs and shakes her head. Anna shifts in her blanket and makes a small yawn, and Mamaw's eyes light up again just as quickly as they had darkened. She begins to hum "Greensleeves."

I look out the window at her backyard. The yard's overgrown but empty, thick with weeds punctuated only by one mimosa tree shedding her pinkish-white flowers into the breeze. The yard goes on and on until it finally ends against the mountainside where it curves up into dirt, twisted up trees and briar bushes. Papaw's garden used to start about ten feet from the porch and go all the way to the back of the yard. I remember the newly planted rows were dark mounds of bumpy earth sprinkled with gray, dry dirt. When the sun had come out enough and the weather was warmer, the plants would begin to come. Soon, the front row would be lined with tomato plants that filled the air with a sour smell that hit the nose sharp like a bee-sting in the skin. Cornrows that reminded me of rotting leaves in wet October smell. There were cucumber plants weaving in and out together with tiny yellow buds flowering around them. To the left, lettuce hugged together pinned inside their chicken wire fence. When I was little I thought since they were called "heads" of lettuce that they had faces under their green bonnet-like petals. Finally, at the back of the garden were the strawberry plants, in small child-mouth shapes, the color of deep red tulips or the red-orange color sunshine turns when you squint your eyes.

I wish he was still out there working in spite of his old bones. I can almost see him now, bent over the tomatoes, picking bugs from their stems, carrying his bucket and hoe, his wide-brimmed hat and red handkerchief hanging out of his back pocket. I imagine Mama taking him a glass of water, back when she was still young and pretty, with that long, almost black hair tied up in a bun. It looked red in the sunlight—that hair I loved to brush before she went to bed. She was muscular and strong. She walked straighter because her limp wasn't so bad back then from all the years she strained her body taking care of me and my brothers and sisters. And back then, Mamaw didn't have *old-timer's* and talk out of her head, rarely making any sense.

Today she is making some sense, remembering an odd variety of things: the accident, her old dog Rusty, and how Papaw liked his eggs cooked. Some days she asks where he is. Today, she remembers he died years ago. Mamaw says, "You seen that little yellow bird that's been nesting in my tree out back yet? She's got her a nest goin'. You can hear her babies chirpin' from the winder. I been givin' her bread crumbs."

"Yeah, I seen her out there just yesterday. She's bright as the day, ain't she?"

Mamaw looks down at Anna and whispers, "That's why we call you Little Bird: because you're bright as the day." She kisses her on her forehead.

I go light lanterns around the house before I head home to help Mama with dinner.

Daddy slaps Isaac upside the head, then leans back in his chair and stares at him from across the kitchen table, his tired eyes shining in his coal-covered face. His body is slumped over in his chair, his black nostrils flaring as he chews. The table wobbles when he brings the fork up to his lips, and he slaps it to stop the motion.

Isaac has his hands on his knees, leering at Daddy, quietly.

"Y'all want some cornbread?" I say.

They don't answer.

"Daddy?"

Daddy grunts.

I lay the bowl on the table and look out the window where orange light sneaks into our plain, brown kitchen. Mama's old hanging plant swings in the breeze on the back porch with one tattered red ribbon dangling from the bottom of it. The wiry vines look like they're praying, the way they bend to the sun over the worn edge of the basket.

Out back, a dusty path starts at our porch steps, cuts through the high, stiff grass and swells before it plunges over the railroad track and out of view. Some yards away I see it peeking above the hills again, up, back down, up again like a giant, smooth snake. Our rotting shed sits off to the left of our house, its roof sagging low like an angry eyebrow above its blank eyes and misshapen open mouth.

Anna May runs in the door, slinging dirt from her shoes the whole way, with Ezra chasing behind her. Anna tumbles. She bumps Daddy's elbow, and his cup falls to the floor.

I bend down to wipe up the mess.

Daddy's blue veins rise like fat worms crawling under the skin of his forehead. His mouth gets tight. Ezra and Anna both stop cold. Anna steps back against the wall. She covers her lips with her hands. Slowly, Daddy rises and stands over her like a mountain. "Your Mama's asleep, and I don't want to hear her mouth if y'all wake her up! Ezra, why don't you act like a man and stop playing with your baby sister! Sixteen and acts like a . . . " Daddy's voice trails off into a mumble as he sits back down in his chair.

"Take me to the creek to make marbles, Jennie," Anna whispers, tugging at the hem of my dress, her big silver eyes blinking up at me. "It'll be too cold pretty soon, and we won't get to go to the creek that much."

"Anna, you shouldn't whine. You should say 'please,'" I say, gently patting her on the head.

"All right. *Pleeeeease*," Anna says, pulling my wrist.

Katie hurries into the kitchen. She rummages through the boxes and bowls on the shelf, pulls down a basket and a cloth to cover it with and says, "Daddy, I'm going over Ms. Hudson's to get some berries. Tell Mama I won't leave the camp."

Us girls start out the room, leaving Daddy and Isaac at the table—Daddy back to stuffing his hard face, Isaac staring a hole through Daddy's black forehead.

"C'mon Jennie, come with me," Katie says, smiling and swinging her skinny arms, grinning like the dog she is. We walk onto the front porch.

Anna huffs and pulls at my elbow. "You said you was gonna take me to make some marbles. You can't go with her for berries, Jennie."

Katie says, "Stop pulling on Jennie all the time, Anna. Good God."

Anna scrunches her nose at Katie.

"Katie," I say. "I know you ain't going to get berries. If Daddy catches you sneaking over to see Jimmy Tucker, he'll beat you half to death."

Katie walks down the front steps of our porch, turns and cuts her chin at me, smiling with those pretty brown eyes. She says, "You're just jealous." She sticks her tongue out at me and walks down the alley. Katie's only fifteen and blessed with chestnut hair, warm toned skin and a doll-shaped mouth. She'll have no shortage of suitors.

Mama says if I hadn't wasted my marrying years chasing Golden I might have made a good match with somebody else. "Fat lot a good thinking about that will do me now," I say out loud.

I stand still, watching Katie walk down the alley lined with houses. The houses are all exactly the same: white with saggy porches and windows dark from coal dust. The sun is going down behind the rooftops.

Anna leads me by my fingers, and we start for the creek.

TWO

Isaac

I'd like to go work for the steel mill. It don't sound hard to say, but more I think of it, the harder it is to tell Daddy. I keep going over it and over it through my head. Ain't got no appetite for supper tonight. Keep running the words through my head: I wanna work for the steel mills, Daddy. Leave here, and work for the steel mills. I'm sick of the coal mines. Steel mills all over Chicago. Aunt Melita and Aunt Mylana moved to New York. Why can't I move away to a place like Chicago?

He's mad at me already. I done something to make him mad as usual. I don't wanna make it worse, but I sure don't know how much longer I can stand living at home. My hands is aching. I almost said that.

Daddy would've slapped me if I had. The table wobbles while he eats. He slaps the corner of the table with his hand. "Need to fix 'is here table, boy," he says.

I just nod.

I keep grinding it through my head: I gotta tell him I wanna leave. I gotta tell him. Finally, he gets done eating and goes out back to tend to his tomato plants. I foller him around the corner of the house and out to the shed. I ain't saying nothing yet.

When we get to the shed he stops, turns around, spits out the side his mouth and says, "What you want? I know you ain't wantin' to help me. You never help around the house."

It just comes out. "Daddy, I wanna go work for the steel mills. I don't like the mines no more, and I figure I could make real good money. Maybe send some back to y'all."

He stands there, gripping a bucket and staring at me.

"I said I figured I could make real good money and maybe I could. . . ."

He spits again and sets the bucket down. "What you figure you could do, boy? You figure you could take care a this family better'n me, huh?"

I put my hands in my pockets. I reckon I shouldn't have said anything. Probably should've just went on out of here without a word. Went and showed him I can make money and that I could help him and Mama out better if I wasn't at home eating up all their food. I just wait. I know what's gonna happen.

"Isaac, you go out there on your own and you ain't gonna do nothing but make yourself look like a fool when you go broke. You can't make it in no steel mill. You stay right here with your family like you're supposed to," he says.

"Daddy, if I could get to a city somewheres I know I could find better work than this."

He pushes my shoulder a little and puts his dirty finger in my face. I can smell the chew on his breath.

He says, "How you gonna get to some city? You gonna fly? Now, do like I told you earlier. Go down and trade that ol' horse. Tell Sam I said just one of them blue tick hounds I traded him is worth more than a horse this old. We need one younger. Come back with a younger horse or them hounds. But don't come back with that old horse."

I don't say anything.

He turns his back to me and starts messing with his plants. I stare.

"Go on," he says, "leave me be and tell your sisters to go down to the store for your Mama."

I go on to get the horse and head down Sam's.

I wanna work in the steel mills. Ain't nothing 'round here. Never will be. I'm a man. Ain't nobody gonna swoop down in this holler, and carry *me* outta here. Hell, I can't see nobody wanting to swoop down and carry my sisters outta here neither. They ain't none of these holler girls *that* pretty.

Guess we'll *all* have to learn to fly.

THREE

Jennie

"It's almost dark," Mama says. "I hope Isaac gets back pretty soon."

Me and Mama sit in rocking chairs on the front porch. Anna is in Mama's lap. Ezra sits on the edge of the porch, swinging his legs and peeling an apple with his pocket knife. Clouds put their cottony heads together, forming a big heap, hunkered over us, shading everything in sight blue-gray.

Daddy sticks his head out of the front door, asks, "That boy still ain't back yet?"

"Give him time, Daddy," I say. "It's a long way Isaac had to walk."

Daddy snorts and goes back inside, slamming the door behind him. I can hear him cussing.

"Days starting to get chilly," Mama says. "Girls gonna need new coats for winter before you know it."

Katie comes walking up the alley with her basket on her arm. The sky grows darker as thunder rumbles, and Katie rushes to the porch.

Ezra turns and looks at me, says, "You figure it took her all that time to get some berries off Ms. Hudson?" He laughs. Anna joins in.

Katie comes up the porch, says, "Look at all these blackberries she gave us. I'm gonna make a cobbler."

A couple of tiny gnats rise from the plump berries as Katie pulls back the cloth to show us, and the sweet smell of blackberry juice and dirt, that rises too.

Ezra grabs Katie's basket, looks inside. "That all the berries you got?" he says. "You was gone a awful long time. Run into anybody else besides. . . ."

Katie pelts him in the arm.

"Katie," Mama says, "what's wrong with you two? Quit it."

Katie smiles at Ezra, all smug, and goes inside.

Mama says, "I don't know what's gotten into that girl."

The clouds crash so loud the house shakes, then they split open like pillowcases spilling out sharp needles of rain that clacks, clacks against our roof. Mama stands up, holding Anna in her arms, and rushes her inside the house, stopping at the door to look for Isaac again. Mama says, "I hope he don't catch his death, Lord willing."

The rain catches its breath, then blows down powerful again.

FOUR

Ezra

Rain eased up some. Just sprinkling now. I go in to get everybody else. I say, "Isaac's coming and Daddy don't look real happy about it."

Everybody comes out to watch and see what Daddy's gonna do. I sit on the porch steps. Daddy stares down the path with his black eyes, waiting for Isaac to get up the alley.

Here Isaac finally comes with a horse following behind him. I know we gonna have to hear Daddy yell, or worse, see him beat Isaac again. Isaac's bigger'n Daddy. I don't know why he don't knock Daddy's head clean off. I would if I was as big as Isaac. Isaac got big arms from all the working he does. I hope to look just like him. Mama wouldn't let me dig no coal before, but now Daddy told her I'm old enough and she needs to shut her mouth 'bout it. I'll be in the mine starting next month. After a few years slinging a pick and a shovel I'll be as big as Isaac.

Isaac comes up to the porch with the new horse. Daddy had asked for younger and healthier. Isaac smiles like he's proud.

Daddy is quiet, just walks 'round the horse, patting its back, and looking in at its teeth. Daddy almost smiles, till the horse throws its head back, and a sound like a cough comes out its throat.

I hear Mama get up from the rocking chair on the porch, and the slam of the door behind her. I don't care. I'm staying right here on the steps with Anna May and Jennie.

"This nothin' but an ol' windsucker," Daddy mumbles. Then, he gets louder. "Old and a windsucker!"

Anna May puts her head down on my lap, and I play with her hair. Jennie tries to get Anna May to go in the house with her, but she won't let go of me.

"I want to see," I say. "Leave us be, Jennie." Jennie sits back down.

Daddy goes on about how stupid Isaac is, and starts smacking him upside the head. "You got this worthless ol' horse when I told you to get one younger! You idiot!" Daddy gets meaner this time. He clenches his knuckles white, and grits his teeth, then he points into the house.

"Get me a gun," he says, his head lowered. Isaac looks puzzled.

"Well, what for Daddy?"

He repeats hisself. "Now."

Isaac goes into the house, and comes out with a gun. His hands is shaking, and he keeps his head down.

"What you gonna do, Daddy?"

I think he thought Daddy was gonna shoot him right then. Daddy raises the barrel, and points it right at that poor horse's face, and he keeps it like that for a few minutes.

Anna May got her face buried in my lap now, and her little hands cupped on her ears, tight. I can't take my eyes off him. What's he gonna do?

Isaac shakes all over. "No, Daddy," he stammers.

Daddy lowers the gun. It's starting to look like Daddy just might change forever. Hell, I might have myself a new Daddy.

I peck on Anna May's head. "Look at that," I whisper.

She raises her face cautiously and takes a peek, then hides her face in my lap again.

Is Daddy gonna start being nice to Isaac? He forces the gun into Isaac's hands. "Shoot it," he says, then spits out the side of his mouth. Well, I reckon not.

Isaac's face is turning all white. Not even white. Hell, he looks almost gray. His eyes look like they drained out all their color. His hands wiggle nervously, trying to hold the gun up at the horse's head. The horse jerks its head back, and makes that dry, coughing noise again. Isaac jumps. The horse sounds like Mamaw May. Like maybe he's got dust stuck in his throat.

"Shoot the Goddamned thang, 'fore I shoot you."

I look at Jennie, and she shivers just like Isaac, but it ain't cold. Anna May is shaking too. I ain't shaking none though. Am I supposed to? I try to. Try to copy their short, jerky movements, but I can't. Does that mean I don't love Daddy? Mean I don't respect him? I think it just might.

I stare at Daddy with my eyes, and try to make them hard, black, and shiny, like his gets when he goes off. I stare at him hard, like Uncle Cletis does when he's drunk and mad at Daddy. He don't even notice me. Just keeps staring at Isaac, and his trembling knees and slack jaw. Daddy screams for Isaac to shoot it one more time.

Here comes Mama out onto the porch. "Don't you dare make him shoot that poor li'l thang! Clem!"

Daddy spits out the other side of his mouth and snorts at her. "You get back in the house! This ain't none of your business!'"

Mama starts swaying, and holds her face in her hands. "Oh, Lord! I can't take this no more. Y'all are killing me," she says.

Daddy gets red in the neck, and his face curls up as he chews. "God damn it!" he spits again, and stamps his foot. "Isaac, just tether the damn thing near the shed." Daddy breathes out that sentence like he might be sick and tired of all of us. I don't care. I know I'm sick and tired of him. I been sick of him.

Anna May gets up like nothing ever happened out here and runs off into the yard to pick a violet, like she knew exactly where it was without looking first.

Daddy goes into the house, cussing at Mama.

Isaac's wide chest rises and falls back down as he sighs heavy. He walks off without looking at any of us, leading the horse, and carrying the gun in his other big hand.

I'd knock his head off if I had them hands.

FIVE

Jennie

When is the rain gonna quit? Anna May lays beside me in bed asleep. I can't help but watch her, the way her little chest moves up and down and her quiet, angel-like face. I'm sure angels must be skinny little children with round faces and half-dollar-sized blue eyes, pouty pink lips that say no evil.

I put Anna May in the only gown she owns: a small white one with long, ruffled sleeves that hug her birdlike wrists. How I wish I had something to curl her hair with, to turn her dishwater blonde hair into streaming circlets of gold. I watch the purple shadows move across her face as she breathes through her tiny nose. She dreams of marbles, maybe chasing rabbits in the hills with Ezra. I hope she ain't dreaming of nothing else.

Mama always told me, "There ain't no where to go for girls like us, Jennie. You gotta love these hills honey, 'cause if you don't, you'll be the saddest girl there ever was." But what did she mean by girls like us?

Ain't we tough as nails, strong as the meanest storm to hit any valley? Can't we scrub, sew and chop wood till our knuckles peel like oranges and bleed? I've seen my Mama's hands slowly twist up like the branch of a rotting tree over the years from all the planting, the packing, the canning, the digging and the cold mountain air that gets in through the cracks of our walls that she tries to keep out with torn newspapers and blankets.

Can't those hands dig through these mountains, build our own road, a road for girls like us? Ain't our skin as thick as a horse's hide? Our backs like the steel shovel Daddy has in the barn? What's she mean girls like us?

Now I don't know what to tell Anna May. Maybe I'd be happier if I loved these hills more, or maybe I'd be just the same. But I want to know what I'd see if I ever climbed to the top of the mountain bordering Blue Diamond and looked over. What I'd see if I climbed even the next one and looked, and the next, and the next. Wouldn't there be something besides valleys if I kept going? What is there besides Caney Branch, West Virginia?

In my dreams last night I imagined two crosses standing tall and white at each side of a wide, black road. The road led somewhere full of strangers, lots of handsome men. I imagined them. All kinds. Tall men with big black eyes, silky hair, and soft hands. Short men with broad shoulders and stiff-brimmed hats, flashy white teeth, and gold watches. Women in new dresses and white gloves, walking with lean, straight strides, their curls shining in the sun.

Anna May grips my finger and twists it. Her large, soft eyes roll like eggs underneath her thin eyelids. She is dreaming. I kiss her cheek, and she slaps me away.

I almost wake her from laughing. "You're even rotten in your sleep," I whisper.

She is dreaming of the rabbits.

The rain pelts against the window like little rocks. Outside it looks like the ground is coughing up dust. The air sticks to my lungs. I breathe in hard, enjoying the heavy smell of honeysuckle that gets riled up when it rains or when the wind blows. The smell of rain makes me want to be in love. Somehow, I know the man I fall in love with will smell like a rainstorm, like the raw, dirty wind.

S I X

Anna May

Daddy and Isaac was fighting over that horse yesterday. They fight all time.

I wanna go over and get a juice from the store but we got to go to Mamaw May's. Why is her skin so rough? Mamaw May coughs and coughs. I wonder if she breathed in some bad air or somethin'? She chokes like that horse does.

Jennie tells me, she says, "Anna May, you give Mamaw a kiss."

I don't like kissin' Mamaw. Her lips is rough, and her breath stinks. It stinks like I don't know what. "Hey Jennie, can we go over to the store, and get a grapefruit juice? Please?"

She says no again. Again!

Daddy puts holes in the cap with a nail so we can't drink it all real fast like gulp gulp gulp ah! When Daddy comes home him and Isaac is all black. There's men that is black like that natural. They black all the time and not from bein' in no mine neither. They live in the camp on down the road a little ways from us. Then there is people that is kinda orange, or red like Mr. Mendez. Mr. Mendez is so nice. He talks funny and, when he talks, he goes, "I no like this, and I no like that." He talks funny. I love Mr. Mendez. He visits Mamaw all the time. Mamaw got lots of friends that talk like that 'cause she used to let 'em stay at her house for money when they'd come from far away to work at the mines.

I got a swing. Isaac put up a swing on the tree in our yard just for me, because Daddy is too lazy, Mama says, to do anythin' for us. If I swing real high, if I stick my toes out, it goes whoosh whoosh whoosh like that. I get dizzy. I wanna go home and I wanna swing.

We're going to Mamaw's today. We'll have to walk real far up the holler where it gets colder 'cause you get up in the mountain where the trees touch each other and that keeps the sun from comin' down on my head. That makes it cold up in the holler. The way the trees are like that over your head and things. Daddy built steps out of dirt leadin' to Mamaw's house. I wonder how he got that dirt to stay like that? When it rains even the steps don't wash away. They stay just like that. Last time we went up Mamaw's, Isaac caught a tree frog: a little green one with sticky feet. It had red eyes. We put it in a cage, but it got out. It went away to be with its friends, I reckon. It had weird eyes like Daddy, Isaac says, or Ezra says or . . . Mamaw May is dying, I think. Catholics—that is, red people and other people who talk like Mr. Mendez—Mr. Mendez says they put a candle in the room and open the window for the soul to get out when folks die. I wanna go to Mamaw May's. I wanna see if her soul flies out the window, or if it takes the door.

SEVEN

Jennie

I feel Mama's thin hand on my leg. "Wake up, Jennie," she says. "We're gonna go see Mamaw May."

Anna pounces on me and says, "We're gonna go see Mamaw, Jennie. Get up! Come see how I fixed the biscuits today with Mama. I fixed 'em. Whew! Your breath stinks!"

I hug her, laughing.

"Come on, Little Bird," Mama says. "Let's leave Jennie be so she can get dressed." Mama leads her back into the kitchen.

The sun has painted the floor and room orange while we slept. Our house is pretty in the morning—and at night—because of the way light and dark moves around everything, distorting the walls and windows so that it's up to your imagination exactly where you are. The house is still cool from last night's rain, and the air easy to breathe. I wish I could just lay in bed. I don't want to see Mamaw May. I don't want to walk so far up the holler. She lives out where it's so quiet you can hear yourself think. Frogs, crickets and the creek are the only things that disrupt your sleep at Mamaw May's. Train doesn't rattle the windows and dishes like it does here. She lives there with all the farmers—where folks still own the land, where the coal company ain't managed to buy them out yet.

When I go there I think about when we lived on the farm. We weren't owned by nobody then. We had to work real hard, but everything we had was ours. Now, anytime the train passes at night I feel it rumble inside my chest, almost like pneumonia. It shakes my dreams, too. I hear it through my sleep just the same as when I'm awake.

I wash my face and get myself dressed.

Katie comes dragging into our room.

"Girl, you look awful," I say. She has a blanket wrapped around her still. "Why ain't you dressed? You been up longer than me. You're coming with us ain't you?"

Her eyes are hollow, and her normally plump lips are chapped and peeling.

"Get dressed," I say. "We got some things to see about, this morning."

Her mouth opens a little, but she doesn't say anything. She doesn't know.

"Katie, Mamaw May is real sick."

"Well, she always is, ain't she?"

I don't answer.

We walk for what seems like forever, up the holler, past Old Man McCoy's house, then the Tucker's farm. As we pass by, Ezra doesn't even think to crack any jokes about Katie and Jimmy Tucker. Nobody says a thing. I listen for the water to get louder as always the closer we get to the crossroads . . . and it does. Anna has dozed off on my shoulder. The steadily growing roar of the creek muffles Anna's quiet snoring.

Me and Katie walk up Mamaw May's porch. Anna May has fallen asleep on my hip. The screen door is crooked and lets Mamaw's cat out easily. The cat must feel the need to leave her be for now. Mama walks ahead of us. We lag behind like wounded soldiers, like Yankees passing through Georgia with no bed to die on. We talk strong, but we ain't strong; not like Mama. She walks deliberately, her chin pointed out, and her eyes straight ahead. We allow her tough Mother-body to shield us from the cool breath of death blowing from the mouth of Mamaw's bedroom.

Mamaw lays in her bed and barely glances at us as we enter. She ain't curled up like she usually is when she sleeps. She lays flat. Her hands are posed on her chest. Eerie, because I know this is how she will lay when we bury her. The hard, black wood around the bed reaches up around her body like the teeth of the devil, and her soft, watery eyes close when she breathes, her body sinking deeper into the bed. Her dried lips curl up on the corners, a good smile for a dying woman. She has lived fine.

Mama always says a good woman is at peace when death comes, because she knows if she worked hard and lived right, the Good Lord'll make all the rest easy on her. Lord tells a good soul when death is coming. He sends it to you, so you can make ready for it. That's how Mama tells it. Don't know if I've ever believed that. Not really.

Anna May wakes, but keeps her head buried into my shoulder. I know she ain't asleep. I think all this scares her. She don't know what's happening. Mamaw opens her eyes every few minutes to look at us and smile, but closes them again as if to rest them. I wonder if she even wants us here in her face like this. Mama sits beside her, holding tight to Mamaw's withered hand. My Mama is losing her Mama. How can she be so quiet about it? I feel like we should do something. Get mad.

Scream. Do something to fight it from coming. But Mamaw seems proud to be dying so quietly, and Mama is proud of her. The room is quiet, dim. There's no fighting or arguing to it. She's taking in death like air. Mama ain't cried a bit. 'Course, I ain't seen Mama cry but once.

There was an explosion up at the mine. The Hudson boys ran over to tell us. We thought Daddy was in it, but he came home just like always. Daddy came through the door and stood speechless when he seen Mama bent over in the rocking chair with her face in her hands and us kids standing helpless around her. That hard look he usually has turned right quick into something I ain't seen on his face since. He took his hat off real slow, laid down his lunch bucket on the chair by the door and went to her. He got on his knee and took her hands in his. They were both shaking. I believe he was surprised anybody was crying for him.

Mamaw looks at me with eyes that seem honey glazed. Katie holds Mamaw's hand while kneeling beside the bed and straining to hear Mamaw's whispery, quavering voice. I reckon I'll go and clean up the house some. Anna May grabs the hem of my dress and follows me to the kitchen.

Mamaw May is so old. It's about time she's let free. I take one of her baskets from the top shelf. She had made one for us girls every Easter until her hands got so tired and curled up she couldn't weave them anymore. I handle it, running my fingers over the bottom and sides. They used to be beautiful, but now they're all wrinkled and dry. There's a knock at the front door. Neighbors already

EIGHT

Mamaw May

I can't hear a word Mary's sayin'. Her mouth's just a movin'. Her eyes are all red and dewy. I wish I could get up from here but can't move for nothin'. The girls is standin' in the doorway lookin' white as can be, like they done seen a ghost. Anna's dress is yellow. Puts me in mind a dress I had when I was a girl. The curtains is yellow too.

I look down and my knees is li'l again. I got li'l knees, stuck out all bony. My legs is wrapped 'round my Paw's hips. He's packin' me in the family room for Mama's wake. They laid her out in a black dress with no frills . . . no pretty stuff. Mama's hands is folded across her, and her bible is stuck in between 'em. Paw puts pennies on her eyes, and I feel myself jerk. Tears come out—too many to hold—and the yellow curtains fly in, wind breathin' through the winder.

She ain't dead yet. She's cryin' and screamin' bloody murder tryin' to push out that child and her sisters is gathered 'round her and I ain't supposed to be in here. Mama cries out. I stay in the corner where it's dark. They can't see me. They won't bother me. I'll just stay here and wait 'til she's done with her business and I'll come out and hold the new baby. I fall asleep in my standin' up position in the corner of the dark room. I wake. Mama's not cryin' no more. I look. I see her there. She's alone and she's quiet. I run to her. "Mama?" Is she sleepin'? Must be awful tired. "Mama?" I'm standin' outside under the tree, and brown leaves is

fallin' down on my face. I put my arms out to my sides
and close my eyes. I spin with my eyes closed. Wind
blows, the sun warms my face. I'm back in Mama's
room and I'm callin' to her, "Mama!" I curl up on her
stomach and look into her open eyes. Her mouth is
open in a "O" shape almost, but just a small "O." I can
almost hear her breathe out one time. "Mama?" I hold
her hand in mine and bury my face in her curly black
hair. She smells like Mama. She feels warm.

I cry into her hair.

"Mama." I feel hands on my waist pullin' me away
from her.

"No! Leave me be! Mama!" I sob.   I hold tight to
her hand, and blue eyes appear under cold creek water
and I put my toes in it. I hear the creek singin' like a
girl, and I sing with the creek.

Mama's eyes are gray and blue like a soft quilt, a sky
about to cry all over the dirt, spill itself over the ground.
I see my children before me. They reach out slow. I
smile. I feel my baby's skin against my face, my first
baby, Mary. She whimpers soft. I smell her new skin. I
feel her warm back against my arm. She puckers her
lips like she's hungry. I close my eyes and fall through
somethin' . . . air.

"Leave me be! Leave me be!"

I hold onto Mama like she's my life, because she is
my life, my only, my love, my Mama. I feel her not
fightin' when Aunt Ester tries to pull me from her. I
hold onto her finger. I hold onto her black curly hair,
wrap my fingers in it and clench my eyes shut. Pray.
Why don't she fight? Fight, Mama. Hold on to me.

I lay down in the leaves below the oak tree. I lay

down and put my arms out and let 'em fall into my open palms until I'm covered in leaves. I feel God kiss my forehead as the first raindrop lands on it. My tears stream down between my cheek and Mama's cheek as I press against her.

I see sun comin' over the mountain, comin' over the top of the church as I turn and look back at it, my hands around my flowers, my weddin' dress gettin' soiled by the mud hole I step in. I feel God kiss my forehead again when another drop of water comes down and is trapped in my veil. My husband holds tight to my hand. He smiles wide, and I see our children somewhere in his smile, his eyes, his handsome face. I touch his mouth with mine.

"Honey, I miss you."

And there I am at his funeral, and there I am under the leaves, and there I am under the rush of tears, of rain under the tree, and there I am warm against my coolin' mother's body, and there I am, and there I am, and there. I feel her soft, curly black hair slip through my small fingers as they pull me away. I breathe out one more time and I . . . let go.

NINE

Isaac

I sit outside around the fire with Ezra. Everybody else is in the house watching for Mamaw to die. "Now Ezra," I say, "people around here just know when it's coming. That's what they say."

Ezra sits squatting, his eyes shining like red glass in front of the fire. Ezra says, "Why all these people show up to watch her die when it could be days? How does anybody know when they're gonna die? Why does she have to remind us to lay her out in her Sunday dress? She don't need to be picking out no dress 'cause she ain't gonna die. There's no way of telling."

I slip a flask of whiskey from my inside coat pocket. I sing the same stupid rhyme I always do.

"Hold this whiskey between finger and thumb, if I leave any, then you can have some!" We laugh. I drink it and give him a drink.

He shudders. "How can Uncle Cletis drink this piss all the time?" he says.

I say, "'Cause Uncle Cletis is as tough as leather, that's why. Man could eat glass, and it wouldn't hurt him." I look toward the house and see Mama standing in the window watching us. I say, "Better quit that cussin' Ezra. Mama got bat ears."

He shrugs, says, "Ah, hell. A man's gotta cuss. She knows that. She ain't been able to change Daddy none 'cause she knows a man's gotta cuss. She don't cuss just 'cause she ain't no man."

"Shut up, Ezra. You sound ignorant as Uncle Cletis. You're sixteen. You'll stop wanting to be like him when you get older, so I just ain't gonna worry 'bout it."

"Know what else?" he says. "I hate that black dress Mama always wears when somebody dies. Makes her look old and fat."

I ignore him and take another drink of whiskey. It's quiet again except for the crickets screaming from the woods and the jar flies buzzing 'round in the dark. I reach up and grab a lightning bug. I open my hands and watch its little black butt light up and go out, light up and go out. Watching it makes me realize I'm a little drunk. Dizzy. I open my hand and it stands on the end of my finger like it's wondering if it should jump or not. It stands there so long not being able to make up its mind I fling it off and watch it spin into the dirt at my feet. "You ever noticed them darn things will get right back up and crawl off no matter how hard you flick 'em?" I say. "How do they do that?"

Ezra shoves a stick into the fire and stirs it around. The embers fly into the air, the wind turning them into a small red tornado up against the black sky.

The wind blows open the screen door, and we both look at it, not really wanting to get up. Just let it blow back and forth in the hard wind. Then it comes like a flood. The first mournful wail pierces the quiet, and the others that start soon after mask the sound of our fire popping, the crickets, and Ezra's short jerky sobs. He looks at me. I just take my hat off and put my head down.

TEN

Jennie

I sit at the kitchen table babysitting all the food the neighbors brought. Mamaw's cat crawls up into my lap, and Anna May still clings to my side. I pet the cat with one hand and stroke Anna's hair with my other. She has her eyes closed and makes little noises like she's sleepy as she sucks her thumb.

Mama walks through the house turning mirrors around and stopping what clocks Mamaw had.

Anna May watches her close. "Why is she doin' that?"

I tell her that's just what they do when folks die. That's how Mama explained it to me when I was a little girl.

Slowly, the house swells with people and the smell of hot rolls, fried green tomatoes, cakes and cornbread. My body just doesn't seem hungry. The neighbors come in and out, the men bow their heads to Mama, holding their hats tight to their chests, and the ladies, in tears, reach out to hug her.

Mr. Mendez comes in with his wife, Rosa. Whenever I see Mrs. Mendez I always stare. She's a small-framed Mexican woman wearing a flowered shawl. She tilts her head to the side, looking at me sympathetically with her large black eyes. I just grin a little, thanking her for the gesture. She reaches a covered dish to me and nods her head.

"You take," she says. I nod back to her. "Thank

you, Mrs. Mendez."

Mrs. Mendez looks so out of place in the middle of this shabby house. She looks like she ought to have flowers in her hair and go floating down the Nile in a boat, but she's here just like the rest of us; trapped and poor. She's too beautiful, I think. She won't live here 'til she dies like the rest of us. She's too beautiful to be buried under the orange clay of some hill in West Virginia. She belongs in a great mausoleum with stone pillars on each side. There should be fresh lawns around her grave and a salt-pepper colored statue of a sad lady in robes who appears to cry each time it rains. I only wish I looked so different. There will be no crying ladies surrounding my grave.

Mr. Mendez goes in to see Mamaw. Me and Little Bird are alone with Rosa. She keeps staring at me and smiling with her arms folded under that black shawl. I put Anna on my hip and follow Mr. Mendez to Mamaw's bedroom.

As we go through the hall and pass two other rooms, Anna's eyes get wide, and she shifts around trying to get a good look at where the voices speaking strange tongues are coming from. A few Hungarians are together talking with Daddy, and he's just nodding, barely understanding their broken English. Anna loves to hear *hunkies* talk. She always stops and listens to them when we go to the company store or church.

"Stop staring," I say. "That's not nice."

Mamaw's room is lined with family. Everyone is talking to each other, and a few people even talk to me as I walk towards her bed, but I can't take my eyes off Mamaw. I begin to wish nobody else was around or that the house would suck me in where I can stay inside the walls for a little while. No one would hear me should I whimper.

Something has changed in her face. She looks younger now. Her cheeks are plump and the color of bread that just rose. Her head is sunk way down into the pillow, and her mouth is half-open. She looks like she's grinning a little. Does God speak to her now? Does the wind carry songs of her ancestors to her? I try to look at death for what it is: cold, nothingness. But I can't look at it that way. If I don't imagine voices of ghosts singing her to sleep, I may die myself, die from the hopelessness of it all.

I remember when I was a girl how I thought she'd be around for the rest of my life. I'd always have her love when the rest of the world was ready to spit me out. I'd always have her voice that came through the air like a feathered arrow when she'd call, "Jennie! Honey, come have some supper!" I'd always have those hands, those hands that now are folded and holding a Bible. No more of her love, hands, or her buttermilk voice.

Something inside me starts to shift for a minute. Heat just courses through my face and eyes; panic. I remind myself I've been through this before. Even now, though, there's a place in me where Papaw was ripped out of my soul. Can't fill it with nothing. What'll I do when my own Mama . . . ? My throat is clenched together. Feels like the pain has got to end because I just can't wake up with this, not every morn-ing I can't. Mama leans over and strokes Mamaw's hair.

"We love you, Mama," she whispers, "and always will."

The faces of my family are like the clocks Mama

stopped the moment Mamaw took her last breath. We are all frozen in time as Mamaw passes above and around us, I imagine, before gracing the blues in the sky and whatever lies outside of it.

Like in after-storm quiet, tears and words I never got to say to her fall from me like rain rolls off leaves.

ELEVEN

Anna May

I shoot the brown rock. It rolls up the board and rolls back. Hits the toe of my black shoe. Our porch is so crooked, but it's good for shootin' marbles.

I'm hot in this dress. It's hot. Sun shines on my head. I think my head is gettin' burnt. My legs is stickin' together. It's hot. *Shew Laws* is what Mama says when it's hot. Shew Laws, have mercy! Now they inside hollering. They saying Lawdy! Whoah Lawdy! They singing so loud. Save her soul! Save it, Lawd! But I thought Mamaw was already saved.

"Stop kicking me, Anna."

"I ain't kickin' you, Ezra. I'm just swingin'," I say. I smack him in the leg. "I'm gonna tell Mama if you don't leave me alone."

"You ain't allowed in there, Anna May. So, you can't go tell Mama. Shut up and shoot your marbles."

I shut up.

Uncle Cletis is wearing a suit. His hair all slicked down behind his ears. Mama is in that black dress. She looks fat in it. Everybody is so sad. They took our picture with Mamaw out here in the yard. We put her in that box. We set her in the yard and got all around the box and stood. Little kids up front 'cause we is little, and big people in the back 'cause they is tall, and Mamaw in the box in the middle with her hands folded and her Bible on her stomach, and she looks mighty poorly. Mamaw looks poorly. In the window I see

Daddy in his good clothes. Daddy holds up Mama so she don't take a fall. Mama falls anyway. She falls down screamin' at the devil, I think. She hollers in words I can't understand.

"Why don't they let us in there, Ezra?"

"We can't go in. I have to watch you. You too little to see folks carryin' on like that Mama said."

I wanna go swing on my swing. But Ezra says it ain't right to swing on no swing while people's mourning in our house. I look in the window. "What they gonna do next, Ezra?"

He says they gonna bury Mamaw in the ground.

Mama come outside.

I ask, "What they hollerin' to save her soul for if she's already saved?"

She rocks me on the swing.

I suck my thumb. I think of the tree frog with its funny eyes and Mamaw, and I listen to them in there hollering Lawdy Lawdy, and I try to go to sleep on Mama, but it's too much noise so I can't. I close my eyes and I wonder when I'll see Mamaw again.

TWELVE

Katie

"It's all right, Katie. We don't have to act like fools on their account. Just ignore 'em," Jennie whispers. She says more. I can't hear half of it for people hollerin', "Praise the Lord" every damn five seconds. I hate church. I won't say it out loud where Mama or Jennie or, heaven forbid, the holier-than-thou Motleys could hear!

Them damn Motley girls. They sit behind us just as pleased as punch to see me and Jennie got on the same dresses we wore the Easter before and the one before that. Mama made all our dresses a few years back, and Anna May was growing out of hers. Mine and Jennie's has a couple of small holes in them. I don't care about no stupid dress anyways. I don't even want to go to church. Sara Motley sneers around, sitting all proper in her little white gloves and her fancy, frilly thing she calls a dress that was, based on her Mama's account (which we heard fifteen times since church began that day) "brought in directly from a dressmaker outside Charleston, South Carolina, which is where our folks is from originally." Why don't y'all just move out there, then? Move in with your fancy cousins, I'd like to say.

The other Motley girl, Tara, just grins like a possum every time Anna May starts to wiggle 'round, tugging at the sleeve of her dress, complainin' how it's too small. I'd like to knock the livin' daylight out of 'em, but seein' how I'm in church I reckon I'll behave myself. Their brother Golden ain't here. He ain't much better than them two. He loved my sister but he's led her on for—what, now?—nigh on five years? My pretty sister Jennie going around passing up perfectly good marriage proposals waiting on that coward Golden, and he ain't even got the nerve to court her just because his family thinks they're too good for us! Damn fool acts all jealous over Jennie to this day. I'm kind of glad he didn't marry her. If he did we'd be kin to snakes. I wish she hadn't passed up them other two marriage proposals, though. Probably won't get married noways now, not at her age.

I can tell Mama's stood about all the carryin' on she can stand. She turns around and very politely comments to Mrs. Motley on how pretty her girls look. She thinks being nice to 'em will make them be nice to us. She don't know no better. "Kill 'em with kindness," Mama says. "Ain't gonna work." I always tell her.

I don't care if Mr. Motley is an engineer, or if his son Golden is sheriff. He and his ain't nobody to me, and I'll tell them that. I sure will.

Even when Mrs. Motley smiles, it still seems like she's looking down her skinny nose at Mama, without even saying a word. Woman won't even speak to her. Like she's too good to breathe in our direction. Mama just holds her head up high when she turns back around again facing front. She looks down at Anna with a cracked smile and tired eyes. She brushes Anna's hair out a her face and, all of a sudden, Anna May stops tugging at her dress. She puts one hand on her knee and grabs Mama's with her other. She looks seriously at the preacher like a little grownup. She tilts her head to the side a bit, listening to him hard for the first time. Mama's smile gets a little wider, more sincere. She draws in breath real deep, shaking a little when she lets it out, and her eyes look a little less tired.

THIRTEEN

Jennie

I sit in class studying my teacher. Mrs. Adkins is a plump woman, with a heart-shaped face and long graying hair she keeps in a bun. I want to be a teacher, but I don't want to seem so bitter like Mrs. Adkins. Sometimes she twists up her face, points her sharp index finger, and yells at some boy to get his feet out of the aisle before she strings him up by his toenails and cuts his gizzards out. I don't think I will use that sort of language if I get to be a teacher. I should get to be a teacher. I've almost finished my schooling.

I hear Sara Motley whispering to her sister Tara, seated just behind me in class. Katie sneaks me a small slip of paper. It reads:

They are talking about jimmy tucker again. Say he's white trash like you and me and our brothers and sisters. I'm gonna wear her out after class. Watch and see.

I write back:

Don't pay no mind to them, Katie. I don't want to get bad marks for conduct. I'll never be a teacher if I get myself into fights my last year of school.

Katie whispers, "Yeah, well I don't want to be no teacher. You just take my books after class and take Anna home with you too so she don't get in no trouble."

Mrs. Adkins peeks out of the side of her eye as if we can't tell she's watching. Lord have mercy, what is Katie going to do after class? Daddy's gonna take the switch to her if she gets in another fight with the Motley girls.

FOURTEEN

Anna May

Jennie don't think I heard her but I did. I heard what Katie said. She said, "What in the hell y'all snobs know 'bout us anyways?"

Books flied everywhere by God! That's when she hit her, when she went *whap whap* and come down like a hammer on her big head. That ugly Motley girl's hair got all pulled out, and she screamed and screamed, and her sister went, "Oh, I'm tellin'!"

And I threw a rock and hit her in her head. "I'll pull 'em ugly weeds off yo' head you don't shut up. I will!" I said. "Hit her again Katie! Hit her again!" I hollered.

Mama says she knows Katie started it but Katie says No, Mama, I didn't start it, and Jennie agrees, and that's when I say, or I was gonna say but then. . . . "Mama," I start out, but Jennie pinches me in my arm. "Ouch!" She put her hand over my mouth and I bit her, but not real hard, only a little. I wasn't gonna say nothin', just ask Mama if she thought Sara Motley's hair looks like red weeds or not.

Me and Katie spend all day doing things together 'cause Mama says she can't stand to look at her right now. We pickin' up the prickly nuts off the ground under the tree and they prick my fingers. I hate that. "I'm tired, Katie. I don't wanna carry yo' bucket no more." The dirt is dark in the mud holes and wet and my shoes mush in it when I walk. "I can't stand fall. Everything dies. It's ugly, Katie. Plus school starts. I hate school!" I holler.

"Oh, hush up. I'll send you to help Isaac clean them squirrel if you don't quiet
down."

But I like guts and I like squirrel. "Yea! I like cleanin' the squishy squishy guts!"

"Now what little girl in the world would like squirrel guts?" Katie says.

Guts ain't no squishier than them boys her and Jennie talks 'bout all time.

"All time!" I say. I stick my tongue out at her.

"Anna, why you always wrinkle your nose up at me like that?"

I don't know why I do that. "Katie, I hear Uncle Cletis tell it that you know a copperhead is close by when you smell que-come-berts. Why is copperheads smell like que-come-berts? Is that what they like to eat? I don't like copperheads a'tall, even if they do smell like que-come-berts. But I sure do like eatin' me some que-come-berts all right.

FIFTEEN

Nandor

Dearest Janos,

I am writing now to you with the English so for you to teach Mama and Papa to our dearest family all it is I have been learning of the English. I listen to the talk of the men I have met on the ship and the tell me of a small place called West Virginia. I am being told by these men they do have much work for us there in the coal mining. There are many houses there for the coal miners to live. It is that I am now going to this place.

I like America. The men are telling me in the place we will be horses are costing much money and it is not every person who has one of these. Even less people are having the motorcars. But there is much work and I will write you soon and tell you of all this new work. I am happy you will all be here with me as well some day. There are many people from our dear Budapest being in this place. I miss you all and love you all. May God bless you and keep you. May our Father in Heaven keep you my dearest family.

Love, Nandi
Sept. 12, 1918

SIXTEEN

Isaac

There's a moan breaking through the darkness and getting into my brain as I sleep. Can't sleep. I wake. I hear popping. Orange light shines into my bedroom. I look out the window. Our shed is in flames and that horse is inside screaming wildly. "Daddy! Wake up, Daddy!" I put on my pants and run out the house barefoot. The flames has already ate half the shed and the horse is beating its hoofs against the door. "Daddy!"

I pump some water from the well as fast as I can and sling the bucket of water onto the shed. It hisses as the water disappears into its hot mouth. What to do? There's nothing to do. Nothing. Did I leave the lantern in there burning? Did I leave it in there to catch fire? That horse is gonna die. Daddy hates that horse anyway. He's gonna kill me. His tools. Our food. All getting ate up by that fire.

"Daddy! Jennie! Katie!" I keep slinging bucket after bucket of water onto the fire. A small corner might go out for a second but the warm night breezes tease the flames back up high and out of my reach.

Finally Jennie comes running out still in her nightgown. "Jesus, Isaac!" She pumps another bucket from the well, and starts to throw it onto the fire. At first I think we're doing some good, but then I hear the front door slam again. Daddy bursts through the front door and runs down the steps with a blanket.

"Daddy I don't know what happened. I just woke

up, and that horse, Daddy, that horse."

Daddy walks past me as if he can't hear me. He shoves the blanket down into the bucket of water, yanks it out, wraps it around him and heads into the shed. A few minutes later he comes out leading the horse. The horse is bucking and kicking until finally it falls over on its side.

I just stand above it looking at it.

Anna May comes running down to it crying, and she pets it up and down its face. "It's gonna die Daddy!" Anna cries. "Don't let the horse die!" She squeals, crying hard, her small fists up under her chin.

Ezra's standing on the porch close to Katie and Mama. They don't move.

Daddy throws the blanket off and walks to me.

"Daddy what are we gonna do about the shed?"

He stops and stares at me. "What do you figure we do? We can't put out this damn fire with two buckets, you idiot!"

I look over to the porch at Mama and Katie and they just stand there in their nightclothes watching us. I look back at Daddy and I can tell he's mad.

"What the hell is the matter with you, boy? You gotta look at them when I'm trying to talk to you?" Daddy looks strange to me. He stares at me, his eyes wide open and eyebrows raised. His face and arms glow orange from the fire raging behind his tall figure. His face is black from the smoke and his teeth look frighteningly white. I've never noticed the muscles in his arms before. The light makes him look powerful and hard. I put my head down.

I don't know what to say. I didn't do it!

Daddy goes into the house and comes back out with

his gun.   He points it at the horse and yells, "Mama, cover them kids' eyes!"

I don't turn my head.

Anna runs screaming up to Mama on the porch.

The horse looks up at me with one walnut-colored eye, its legs flailing and black nostrils flaring. Seems like everything is going slow now.

I wanna kill Daddy. I wanna take his neck into my hands and I wanna . . . . All I can see is my hands going for him and his stunned face. He looks so old now. He drops the gun. His wrinkled face turns white in surprise, and it's too late now. Now I gotta beat him down. It's just too late Daddy. I don't want to, but he'll kill me if I don't kill him. He'll kill me, Mama. "You've always hated me!" I scream at him, and I pull him up to me close with my hands on his shirt almost strangling him. "You hate me!" I spit out words in his face, and he looks frightened and somehow it makes me angrier. Him being scared makes me angrier. Fight back! Hit me like you always do! Hit me!

Mama starts screaming, and Jennie. "Stop it! No, Isaac!"

This is it. This is what will rip us all apart finally. I reach up with my free hand and hit him hard in the jaw. His face is stunned. His expression is froze. His eyes look like the horse's eyes, and I fight him as hard as I can. Finally he starts to fight and he hits me once in the mouth. I push him down onto the ground, and I hear him cough almost like he does mornings, and this hurts me. It makes me not want to do this. I get on top of him with my hand raised, and his face quivers, and he covers his face to protect himself, and all my weight is holding him down.

Jennie screams, "Isaac! Stop!" from somewhere. She grabs my wrist with both her hands. That's not enough to stop me, but I do. I stand up, wiping my hands on my knees. I just stare down at him.

He won't get up. He lays there covered in dirt. I touch my cheek. I had no idea I'd been crying. I look at Jennie. Her entire baby-doll face looks scared of me or sorry for me. I don't know which. I see Mama still standing on the porch. "I'm sorry!" I scream. Over and over. "I'm sorry!"

Mama didn't sway like she was gonna faint or nothing how she does usually. Mama didn't move. Mama was standing, and Daddy was lying on the ground.

I run. I jump the fence and run out into the dark woods.

SEVENTEEN

Jennie

Deep voice booms, echoes through the valley, chases me. "Jennie!" His voice is not my father or my brother or any of my kin. "Jennie!" Sounds like a woman in pain and a man chasing the wife that does not love him. "Jennie!" Sobbing my name. Sobbing.

The numbness climbs up through my bare feet and up through my calves. I run. I run hard. I'm falling. I keep running clean through the arms of willows grabbing at me, briar bushes slapping me, cuts burning! Sun glaring above trees, green fingers blocking my view, slinging balls of light out of the sky and into my face. Jumping over ditches and fallen branches like I don't know where I am going. I don't. I don't! Closer to death. Closer! I keep on. Covered in mud. My feet bruised, bleeding. Ignoring the pain. Just can't get far away enough from the voice. Keeps reaching out to strangle me with its cold hands. This is blame. I trip over a rock, spin into mud, my face buried. I look up. I see my father's face slung by some unseen force against a black wall. It knocks him out. His eyes roll back in his head, the whites glaring in his black, coal-painted face as he slips underwater. Suddenly, I am slipping underwater.

"Daddy!" I'm falling, suddenly. Daddy is drowning, and I'm drowning. There's no air. I can't breathe. "Daddy! I can't see! My face is so cold! I'm so cold!"

I hit my head on the ceiling and feel water enter my

mouth.

"Jennie, wake up. Wake up, Jennie."

I cry into Katie's arms. I glance out the window. Lightning pours light onto what looks like a woman in Mamaw's clothing standing under the willows only yards from our house, her palms upturned to the rain. Lightning crashes again, and the vision is gone.

Katie rocks me.

Anna stands wide-eyed at the foot of my bed, afraid of my delirium.

EIGHTEEN

Jennie

I sit on the front porch steps sewing, the sun beating down on my legs. Anna is sprawled out on a blanket next to me, reading. Daddy's splitting wood for the new shed. We missed church today because Mama was too upset to go. Neighbors pass by on their way home from church still in their Sunday clothes, staring at Daddy. They're all talking about us, I'm sure, what with all the noise last night.

"Jennie," Anna says. "Katie said we're lucky to be white, 'cause if we was in the black camps or the hunk camps we wouldn't have yards big enough to build sheds in."

"Oh, she did?" I say.

"Yep, she did."

Suddenly, Isaac and Golden come walking up the alley together.

Daddy's lips get tight and he starts scratching his neck, takes his hat off, puts it back on, scratches his neck again. He glances at Isaac, then at the wood, then at Isaac. Isaac keeps his hands in his pockets and almost acts like he's going to turn around and leave. "How are you, Golden?" Daddy says.

"I'm okay, Clem. Heard you had a fire last night. Everything fine now?"

Isaac and Golden sort of linger at the fence. Isaac puts his head down and kicks a little dirt with the toe of his shoe.

Daddy sighs, nods and says a few words. I don't even hear him. I continue running the fabric through my fingers, but I can't sew. Every few seconds or so Golden looks at me with a strange, sad face, not like he's wounded exactly. He has the expression of someone at a funeral who doesn't know the deceased but who loves and wants desperately to comfort the most grieved mourner.

Do I have to stare? I try to turn my eyes away, and I do, but I can't for long. I just have to see. My stomach twists and turns like the thread around my finger. "Shoot, I broke my thread," I say.

Daddy props his ax against the fence. Golden comes into the yard and Isaac comes behind him, cautiously.

I say, "I hate to use this brown thread in your pretty white gown, Little Bird. When I get some white thread I'll take it out and do it again."

She rolls over on her side holding her book upside down with her hair streaming over the top step. "I don't mind" Anna says, "if it's white or brown."

I take the book and put it right side up for her. She giggles. I pat her head.

Daddy says, "I figured you'd be making your way back here. Don't stand there. Help me get this shed started."

Isaac looks at Daddy for just a minute and then lowers his head again.

The door opens, and Mama comes out on the porch. "Clem!" Mama yells from the porch. "Don't you dare let that boy chop wood! He's been out the whole night! Probably dead tired. He's liable to cut a finger off!"

Daddy just shakes his head as Mama goes to Isaac. She takes a handkerchief out of her dress pocket and starts to wipe his face. Golden almost laughs. As soon as he looks at me, I'm surprised when he keeps smiling. I smile a little back. His smile makes me hurt and want at the same time.

"I'm all right Mama," Isaac says.

"Where was you the whole night?" Mama asks him.

Daddy groans, "Leave the boy alone for Christ's sake."

Mama marches over and sticks her finger in Daddy's face.

"Mary," Daddy starts, now pointing his finger right back at her. "You're starting already. At this hour in the morning! I tell you what, I. . . ."

Mama just stuffs the handkerchief in her dress pocket and walks up the steps like Daddy isn't even talking to her. The door slams behind her. I want to laugh, but no one else is, so I don't.

Daddy's neck is blood red. He turns to Golden and throws his hands up, says, "I swear to God if that woman shut up for ten minutes I believe she'd die of loneliness not hearing her own voice." He points at the house. "I don't see her out here chopping this wood. Says she's sick, you know, but you take that woman to that snake handling church a-hers and she'll roll down the damn aisle like a . . . a. . . ."

"Daddy," Anna says very seriously from behind her book. "I don't think they do that at Mama's church."

I sputter trying to hold my laugh in.

Daddy slings his ax into the wood. "God damn it," Daddy says. "Y'all just leave me be. I'm going in the house. When the woods done chopping itself, will you tell it to make itself into a new shed?"

Isaac sighs and Golden pats his back. Isaac laughs and takes the ax and begins the work Daddy abandoned. Golden stands with his back to me now, watching Isaac. I hear him say something about needing to get back to his own business, which is patrolling Caney Branch. I remember when he used to come to see me and we'd sneak around together when he should've been on duty or at home sleeping. I remember when I thought he loved me because of how he kissed me, and I remember the sound of his voice when he said, "I don't love you." All I could think to say back was, "I didn't ask if you did."

NINETEEN

Isaac

I seen that crow yesterday, and a couple days before that, too. Come up behind me yesterday when I was riding past the crossroads and flew straight over me. Now, there it is sitting on the fence again. "Look, Jennie! Look before it runs off!" I say and point at the thing as it struts back and forth. "Look at him, sticking his stupid beak up in the air like some kind of smartass. I ought to shoot that thing."

"Isaac, you're not right in the head, you know that?" Jennie says, laughing.

"I'm serious, Jennie! That damn crow been following me! I think it must be some kind of sign. Probably telling me there's something bad 'bout to happen."

Jennie looks up at me from her quilting. I hope she's making that quilt for me this time. Mine got so many holes in it. It's getting colder out, too.

"Good Lord, Isaac. I never seen the beat! Why, you sound like Mamaw May, talking all that nonsense about birds warning you somebody's gonna . . ."

I interrupt her. "Don't say it, Jennie, or something bad might happen!"

Jennie laughs. "Would you shut up, Isaac. Mama! Isaac's ruining my quilting out here!" She laughs again.

Mama hollers from inside the house, "Isaac, leave your sister alone!"

Okay, fine. I'll be all quiet for now. "Stop snickering, Jennie." I flip her in the ear. "Ouch! Mama!"

TWENTY

Isaac

Me and Daddy inside the mine. Canary sitting still on its perch inside the wooden cage next to Daddy's feet. He helps me put up a curtain. He looks at the bird every now and then, nods when he wants me to move out of the way. He sets up a shot. Nothing shows but the white of his eyes and the mild glow of our carbide lights. The yellow of the bird. Cold water drips every few seconds from the ribs above us. It's in-the-womb quiet. Like something inside here is alive but asleep in the dark somewhere. Can't see it. Can't feel it. Just the breathing of the tunnel. The air is stagnated. It hangs heavy around my neck.

"They shouldn't have us down in here with all the raining it's been doing. That dam bound to bust some-time, and here it's been raining for three days." He always says that after a big storm. "I heard they let a woman in this mine not too long ago. You know it's bad luck a woman being in a mine? Why, they was twenty men got burnt up in a explosion the very day af-ter a woman went down in that Amherst mine." I just shake my head. I never heard of that story except from him. He likes telling creepy stories sometimes when we're down here. I don't think it's funny.

The air in here is cold and somehow seems to grow warmer for a moment like something is coming. Prob-ably just daddy's ranting and raving 'bout the water getting to me is all. He can't be right. Water coming down here from above ground is too much to think about right now.

Rats pitter past us, red eyes glowing in the dark. My heart sinks into my gut. I know rats don't run for nothing.

"Daddy, let's get!" I holler.

Before we jump up from our knees, our carbide lights flicker as the tunnel rumbles.

The canary screams, flaps wildly from its perch and out of our room.

Daddy drops a stick of dynamite in the black dust and I hear it make a small noise echoed through the cave, quickly taken over by a roar, almost like storm-wind. My own heavy breathing as we run. And distant screams of miners. This is not how I'll die.

TWENTY-ONE

Jennie

Katie and me walk down the long staircase of the company store. I carry nothing and Katie totes a bag of meal on her hip like it's a baby. Golden and his deputy, his half-wit cousin James, stand at the bottom of the stairs. I feel my breath stifle in me. My stomach moves like Golden just ran his fingers across it.

"Some sheriff he is," Katie says. "Hangin' 'round all day doin' jack shit."

"At least he's helpin' out the men tryin' to start up the union around here. That's dangerous for him to do."

Katie almost growls at me. "That ain't no proof he ain't directly kin to snakes," she says. "Look at him, the smartass, good lookin' and knowing ever bit of it."

I hate that he's so handsome. It's the only thing I like about him, and I'm going to keep telling myself that until I believe it. He leans against the banister, smiling and giving one quick wink. When he smiles, a feather could knock me right over. After three years, he still wants my attention like he doesn't get enough from other girls.

Katie trips over Golden's foot. She slides in the dirt palms first. The bag of meal flies, and hits the ground splitting itself and showering Katie! It's like everything has stopped. I see her bleeding bottom lip and the way her breath shows up in the cold air. Her cheeks are red. That ain't from the cold.

"Katie girl, let me help you up!" Golden says. "Are

you hurt bad? Lord, I sure am sorry." I've never heard him sound so sincere since the time he told me he was sorry about hiding me from his family. He must know my sister can and probably will slap his face, sheriff or no sheriff. She stands, fists clenched, red faced. Oh, boy. Here we go. She swings at Golden, hitting him right between the eyes. He covers his nose and grabs Katie's wrist. "Now, you just calm down there! Don't you hit me again! I was just playing!"

I pick up the bag. Useless. Meal covers the wet ground. I shake the dust from the back of Katie's dress.

"My lip's all busted," she says. I would almost like it if she hit him one more time. Instead, she walks off, and I follow.

"Sons of bitches," Katie says under her breath.

I look back at them as we walk away. There's still that string inside me he tugs anytime I see him. "Sorry about your lip, Katie Dawn," I say. "You the only girl I know would hit a sheriff."

She spits. "I can't believe you almost married that fool," Katie says.

I cringe but don't say anything.

TWENTY-TWO

The Creek

I have been let go. I collected for years behind the dam, it has rained for days and days. The dam has burst open like stiches on a wound, like a gate to Hell and now I come down and down. I'm leaning to the right and around the bend and further into black. Need someone to come to, someone to give myself over to. Want something to wrap around, and I sense them. The men are clawing at the walls, flailing inside me. Forty-five, sixty, seventy-three. I quiet the screams. Men and young boys all in black suits, taken up and left floating behind.

I see a black man. His eyes shine in the dark. I see his teeth and tongue when he screams out at me, his palms outstretched. He drops his pick and shovel, turns, runs. I slip beneath him, pick him up. He swims inside me a moment and, then, nothing.

I pick three more. I slam one of them against the tunnel wall. He's out before he realizes what I am. He floats along with me and the other one hundred or so men I have taken down so far. I tumble like a wave over them all. Screaming and more screaming. There is no need to scream. I quiet them as I rush for the ones ahead—some crawling, some running. I quiet them all. The small ones, the sixteen year olds and the six-feet-tall, two-hundred pound brutes. None can run faster than I come.

A kid, maybe fourteen, stands still, shivering, holding his cap tight to his chest, clenching his eyes shut as his

cap slides from his fingertips to the black dirt below. I
hit his knees hard, pull him down and listen to his prayers about his brothers, his mommy and his daddy who is
further down in the mine. I listen. Then I whisper
something to him. I think he hears me because he stops
fighting and lets me carry his body through the tunnel.

All washed clean. All taken. I rise from the floor
and up to their waists, and I pour into the next section,
and here stands a father and a son. Son reaches out his
arm as if to stop me.

"Isaac!" The father screams.

I slide past them, only surrounding their ankles at
first. Slate loosens from above and falls on us all. I am
trapped here for now. They are trapped. I'm rising
above them slowly, looking for a way to get out. Blood
trickles down the son's left eye. The father lets his arms
float as I take him. He leans back a little, his breathing
flimsy. Isaac pants, touching the top of the tunnel now
as I lift him clear off his feet. Father's eyes blink as I
reach them as if he can keep me from coming into
them. I come into his eyes, his suit, his body. Peeling . .
. I peel at them both. The father reaches out to grab the
Isaac's arm. He grabs it tightly as they hold their faces
up to kiss the slate above, to breathe where I haven't yet
reached.

"I love you, Isaac! I love you, son!" He yells weakly
over my roar, gasping.

Isaac's eyes grow wide as he breathes a shallow
breath.

A wooden cage rises to the top. A small canary flies
out, and I shove her bright yellow body against the slate
along with the men's faces, and I come up around their

eyes and up around their noses.

Inside me, Isaac looks into his father's face, and his father looks into his as they both struggle to hold their breath. Their limbs move slower now and their hair sways in my motion. I have found a crack through which to slip and, slowly I begin to lower, but I'm too slow. Their eyes are wider now. I want to let them go. I realize I cannot.

The father gives up first—opens his mouth and breathes me in willingly. Isaac's mouth forms an "O" shape in a scream I'm sure would've had tears had I not been here.

TWENTY-THREE

Katie

"I can't believe he tripped me. What a peckerwood. I . . . ," I say.

"Hush!" Jennie interrupts me, reaching for my arm and squeezing. "You hear that?"

I strain to listen. "I don't know. Just sounds like somebody's dinner bell to me."

"No, that ain't no dinner bell. Listen."

It dongs again. Silence. Then again, again, again, again. Something is happening.

"Let's go! It ain't stopping!" Jennie cradles the busted bag of meal on her hip as she runs yelling for me to follow. We run home as fast as our legs can carry us, breathing in that cold air so deep it makes my nose and lips go numb. The sound continues. I grab my dress and lift it so I can run faster. We tramp through half-way frozen mud holes in the front alley of our camp. I notice every sagging porch is full of women and small children hugging their Mama's or sister's legs. Some have babies in arms but no one is moving, it seems, except for us. We run up the front steps of our house and fly through the door.

"Mama! Mama, what is it?" Jennie says.

I follow her into the kitchen, panting, hands on my knees. Anna May is on Mama's lap. Mama rocks her, staring off into space as she hums.

"Mama, what's happening!" Jennie says, more of a demand than a question.

Anna sucks her thumb and looks up at us and the back at Mama. Mama tucks Anna's hair behind her ear.

Anna wiggles, then brushes her hair back to how it was.

"I'm sure your daddy ain't in it. He nor Isaac," Mama says, with no real emotion. I don't believe her.

I sit on the floor in front of the coal stove so long the heat starts sting my back.

Jennie looks awful worried.

"Jennie, honey, Mama's telling you sit still. Running around like chickens with our heads cut off ain't gonna help. We'll go on down yonder in a bit."

I'm just staying quiet. Last time we all was scared, turned out Daddy was fine and we was all tore up for nothing. They probably ain't in it.

Jennie paces, popping her fingers and wrists over and over. Hate it when she does that.

Mama rocks Anna.

I reckon we'll sit a spell, then go hunting for 'em after while. "They probably ain't hurt," I say.

I say it to myself in my mind. They ain't hurt. My daddy nor my brother. But I don't really believe it.

TWENTY-FOUR

Coal Dust

I slip down from the tipple in the center of the camp. I was scraped out of the earth, and now I fall from the sky. Wind moves her hands around me like she polishes me, but I don't come clean. No, I'm black, and whatever I touch I make black. I go now to stick into lungs, to cover the camp in a thin veil of black. I snow. I drift down to color the white houses a smoky shade of gray, to fall like leaves into the cracks of rooftops, to nestle in a young girl's hair, to be cradled in the threads of an old man's coat. I glide. I'll glide until I find somewhere to stick or someone to breathe me in.

Below, dozens of rooftops, and women stand in the dirt alleyways between their homes. Women wailing, babies in arms. Why do they wail? Why do they cry?

I'm lifted and pulled. I spin in through a window, up toward the ceiling and slowly down again.

A young girl paces around the house—screaming, pulling her hair. She stomps. She pounds the walls with her fists. I can't understand her words.

Another girl sits in the floor with her green dress spilled about her. She cradles and rocks a little girl. They each have tears hanging from their chins, slipping down their necks. She covers the child's ears with her hands. She screams, "Katie, please stop! Mama! She's scaring Anna! Mama, make her stop! Please!" The little girl cries a hard cry that almost sounds like a laugh as she tries to say something.

The mother sits still in a rocking chair with her hands folded neatly on her knees. Her eyes are blank, large.

Tears pool in them but don't fall. Then she blinks, and they pour down her face. She takes in a breath that pulls me near her. I descend softly into her hair unnoticed. I tremble as she trembles.

TWENTY-FIVE

Jennie

I can't stop looking at Daddy's hands. Isaac's are all bloated, too.

Mama's sitting next to me in the family room.

We got them both laid out in their Sunday best. I don't understand it seeing as how neither of them would've stepped a foot in church, but I guess it's just custom to do it that way. I notice there's a crow perching on our window sill.

Mama don't move next to me. She's just still and quiet. I wonder if she even feels her own hand covering her eyes.

I want to say something, but I don't.

She blinks real slow. She rubs her hands together, turns them over, looks at her palms. She seems to inspect her nails. I don't really know for what.

Katie is on the other side of her. Their arms are locked together. She rubs Mama's back. Katie looks mad. She always looks so mad when she's thinking hard or even just doing something repetitive like sewing or washing clothes. She's got all the anger all the rest of us girls in the camp know we got to hold in. All the wives hold their anger in long after they give birth to baby girls they may or may not have wanted to have to begin with and them those girls grow up to be angry, too. Lot of angry women around here. I'm sad a lot, mostly. For our family, for myself.

Will we ever have a mattress burning at our place now? Not mine. Not until Anna's grown at least. Not without Daddy and Isaac around to help Mama.

Katie sobs and sobs.

I can't look at anyone. I can't look.

I run my fingers through Anna's tangled almond hair streamed across my lap. She sucks the tip of her thumb. Breathes loudly through her nose as she rocks herself a little. I know she's just doing this so not to cry.

Nothing I know to do for myself. I let it fall from me. I keep myself up straight. I'll sit up straight. My face is hot. My throat aches and closes.

Ezra

I don't want to go in where they got Isaac and Daddy laid out. Ain't no damn sense in it nohow. Why they got to lay them out anyway? We know what they look like. The water must've been extra cold on them because they look a little blue. Or maybe all dead folks look like that. I wonder how far Isaac floated. If they found him right away or if he was stuck in that hole for a long, long time. . . . Why is this the shit I'm thinking of? Why does it matter to me how long they floated or where they did or didn't them? They're gone and there's nothing any of us can do about that. I don't cry. I'm a man and we don't stand around like women and cry. My sisters are crying.

I'm going to just sit here quiet just like Isaac would if it was me laying there instead of him. He wouldn't want me carrying on like a sissy.

Jennie walks out of the room and closes the door behind her, holding Anna. Anna's crying real hard. Jennie says, "You gonna sit with Isaac a little while, Ezra? There ain't nobody else in there right now but Mama and Uncle Cletis if you. . . ."

"No, why don't you leave me be? I don't want to go in there. It's just a dumb ol' wake. People standing around staring at them. Ain't no point in that"

Anna stops crying so hard.

"Well at least get up out of the floor and sit in a

chair. Somebody coming out here'll step on you," Jennie says.

"I'm fine in the floor. I like it in the floor. Why you bothering me about every little thing, Jennie? Ain't you got things to do? Go do somethin' girls do. Fix Anna's hair somethin'."

Jennie stands there looking down at me a few more minutes, and then Katie comes out, and the door hits me. "I told you somebody was gonna hit you with the door. Get out of the floor, Ezra." She says that quiet.

"No you didn't, Jennie. You said somebody was gonna step on me."

Katie is crying a little bit and puts her arms around Jennie and Anna.

Anna calms down.

"Jennie, we really should get Anna cleaned up," Katie says.

Anna shakes her head no and rubs her eyes. "Sleepy," she says.

"See, she wants y'all to leave her be, too. I'm gonna go sit on the porch. Y'all tell Mama if she asks for me."

"Ezra, it's cold out," Jennie says. "You come sit by the coal stove with us. We're gonna eat some cake. You want some cake, don't you? Aunt Melita made it."

I cross my arms, and somebody else comes out and whacks me with the door. "God damn! I wish y'all would stop hitting me with the stupid door!" I holler.

It's Uncle Cletis. "Sorry, Ezra," he says, "Didn't know you was sittin' there."

Katie slaps me against the back of my head.

"Damn! Why did you do that!?" I say, rubbing the back of my head.

"For cussing like a sailor. Mama's gonna hear you,

stupid."

"Katie, don't call him stupid," Jennie says.

"Well, he is stupid!" Katie says.

"No I ain't!" I stand up. I'm going to go outside and sit by myself.

"Katie, you ought not a said that to Ezra," Jennie says.

"A man's gotta cuss, Katie!" I holler as I walk away.

TWENTY-SEVEN

Jennie

I sit on the top step of our front porch thinking, *I just buried my Daddy and my brother.* I can't get up to change my black dress. Anna's laying with her head in my lap and a thick quilt thrown around her. She should go inside. It's still too cold for her to be out in this weather. But I don't make her. I look around at the dead grass, all wiry and brown, and up at the willows in our front yard. The whole day's overcast with this gray color like God spilt the water he cleans his paintbrushes in, soaking his whole canvas in dreary shades. I sigh.

Mama's inside in bed. I reckon she'll be there the rest of the day. Now, when she walks, her limp is much more noticeable. I fear she's gonna need a cane before too long. I can't stand that limp. It makes me mad somehow. Her hands are always hurting her. This makes me mad too.

I pet Anna and notice her eyes are open. She's staring off at nothing. I hum to her. I sit quietly, watching another new family moving in across the alley. Mexicans. Katie is upset they've been moving foreigners into the white camp. Nothing we can do. Too many men died in the flood. Now the company's putting new folks in wherever they can fit them even if they don't "fit." I hear them speaking Spanish from over here. I recognize it from hearing Mamaw's neighbors when they visited. Donald Smith died in that accident, too, and here they are, already putting his family out and a new family in. The superintendent ought to be ashamed. I don't see how that man sleeps at night, the way he treats folks like they don't count.

To him I reckon they really don't. Every human is just another pair of hands to make him a dollar. He acts like coal miners ain't got mouths needing fed or a brain that knows it. Another thing the company thinks people ain't got is eyes. People around here know what's being done to them and men won't stand for it forever. Not by how I hear men talk, especially now that so many have died. Company wants them to work fast as they can and not worry about being careful. They don't care if the mines is safe. They'd kill my whole family if they though they could sell our blood for a nickel. So much hate growing in my heart. All hail King Coal.

A sliver of sunlight pierces through the clouds and moves across the ground and then the boards under my feet. I can see Daddy when I close my eyes, sleeping in the sunlight Sundays. How many times I've found Daddy asleep in the rocking chair on this porch. I'd always find him sitting straight up with his mouth open and our old dog Buster wrapped around his feet.

When I see that banister, I remember my aunts Mylana and Melita back when they lived close enough to visit more often than just on Christmas and Thanksgiving. I remember when I was a little girl and they'd stand around on this porch and sing for no particular reason, with Mama and Mamaw May. I must've been only five or six, standing up to their waists. My little cousin Yvonne and I would sit here and watch them sing songs about the Lord, and we'd try to join in. I didn't like the way my voice crowded in on their perfect harmony, so I'd sit there and just listen. Yvonne never could sing without smiling. This always made me laugh because she had the biggest smile with these real deep dimples, not something you could ignore, especially at a funeral. She never was allowed to sing with the aunts at family funerals for everybody fearing she'd smile like a possum through the whole thing. There's a certain way to act at a funeral and smiling the whole time ain't it. Only person allowed to laugh and carry on at funerals is Great Aunt Betsy 'cause she's seventy . . . and a drunk.

On summer days we'd have family reunions and everybody would bring their best dish: fried chicken or mashed potatoes with gravy and always Daddy's barbecue ribs. Aunt Mylana would start in on some sad old song, then Aunt Melita would follow her lead, and there Yvonne would start in with her pretty little voice. Her voice was steady and soft among the hearty wails of my aunts, the deep, religious kind you hear in church Sundays that makes you want to cry or reminds you of a relative that has passed on.

"We need to see your mother, young lady. Tell her it's John Black, Detective."

I look up, woke from my daydream. He wears a dark suit and shiny black shoes. He stands in front of me with another man. Behind them two others sit holding long automatic rifles. Company thugs. Neighbors crack their doors to peek out. Mexicans from across the alley go inside their house. I can see their shady figures looking out at us from behind their screen door. I wouldn't come out neither if I was them.

I stammer for words.

Anna gasps, jumps up and runs in the house, the screen door slamming hard behind her. Mr. Black doesn't react. He's stone-faced.

"Mama, there are some men out here for you!" I holler.

Mr. Black looks about, tapping his foot. Over his shoulder I see Mr. Hernandez tiptoeing onto his porch and down the stairs. He comes near to watch. His small son cowers behind him. He motions for the boy to get inside. The sunlight glistens on the pistol at his side.

Mama comes outside. She has no expression on her face at all.

"Ma'am, as you know, this house is Company property. When an employee of the Company terminates service the premises must be immediately evacuated," he says calmly. "These men will help you get your things."

All three men go into our house. Just as fast as they went in they come out carrying different pieces of our furniture and they set them on the ground outside. I don't understand how they can do this. Where do they expect us to go? Mama sits down next to me. She pats my leg and sighs.

Katie swings open the door, glaring at Mr. Black with steady eyes. Her hands are fists at her hips. She don't shiver a bit.

"Katie, you come here," Mama says.

Katie teeters back and forth a little, wringing her hands. Oh Lord, little sister, please don't say a word. I know Katie has the devil in her like Daddy. What's she going to do? "I think y'all need to get the hell off our property." It rolled off her tongue. Holy shit. Why couldn't she just tell him Ezra works for the mine now so they'll go and leave us alone?

I can't speak. I can't say anything. Say something, Jennie. Why can't I open my mouth?

The men pause and Mr. Black waves his hand for them to continue. They do, and Mr. Black walks over to Katie slowly.

"You don't touch my little girl," Mama says, coming to her feet.

Mr. Black starts slowly toward Mama.

Katie moves between them, only falling into Mr. Black's grip as he snatches up her wrists. "Our daddy and brother just died, and here you are to collect your stupid house just after we bury them. Don't even give folks time to grieve proper. You're a lowdown dirty bastard, and I want y'all to burn in hell," Katie says in a chillingly calm tone. She spits on him, and he slaps her.

I pull her away, nearly knocking us both down. Katie falls quiet but pants, leering at Mr. Black as if she'd like to kill him. He just wipes his face with a handkerchief from his coat. I don't know why they ain't shot us yet. I can't handle seeing a man's hand raise in anger. Reminds me of Daddy before he quit drinking.

A scene from my dreary childhood flashes in my head, and I see three-year-old me standing in the kitchen and watching Daddy beat Mama with his belt. I stand in the corner, invisible, my body sinking back into the wall where I don't have to watch or feel. I close my eyes as if trying to squeeze the memory out of them. I want to keep them closed. I fear I may open my eyes to see Mama curled in the corner on the floor not crying, not screaming, just covering herself with her arms as Daddy screams curses and gets madder. I learned to not cry, too. I learned to not make any noise when I do cry. Tears surround my eyes, but I swallow, imagining

I'm in the wall again. My face is cold.

I notice our neighbors are on their porches watching. "Hello," Mr. Hernandez says. "These people are having boy who is still work for mine."

"Who the hell is this? Want to move today, too, Mister?" Mr. Black says.

"My name Hernandez. My family move here this few days." He's not a bulging, strong man, but lanky, old. Why, a heavy wind could knock him down. He looks straight into Mr. Black's eyes when he talks. Sounds so sure of himself. He carries himself like he's somebody and you better know it. I respect him immediately.

"That true? Still have a son living, working for the company?" Mr. Black asks.

"She does," I say.

Mama nods her head yes but doesn't speak.

"Expect this to be the last time you treat a detective this way, little girl," Mr. Black says, eyeing Katie. "Fine. You can stay for now. Boys." He motions for the others to follow him. They leave our furniture in our yard and pile back into the motorcar and slam the doors. I feel his eyes burning on me, on my sister. I know they'll remember this. We all stand still, watching the car disappear in the dust. I think everyone's wondering what to say next. We look around at our furniture sinking in the grass.

"I sure do appreciate you doing that." Mama says, walking down the steps. Mama shakes his long hand. She seems to come out of her statue-like state and smiles warmly for the first time in days.

He looks a little surprised at her smile but he gives a

smile, too.

"It's awful nice to have good neighbors. I appreciate it. Sure do. You come on in now and let me wrap up some cornbread for you to take to your misses," Mama says.

Katie looks at me surprised.

He smiles at us girls as Mama shows him into the house.

I notice Golden walk by just then, tipping his hat. I look the other way, on down the front alley in the direction the thugs went. For some reason, I see them coming here again. This feeling makes me feel cold. I shrug off the cold the same way I shrugged off Golden. Every day I get better at ignoring him. "You're worse than a truck load of dynamite, Katie. Don't try nothing like that ever again. Next time them men'll have our hides," I say.

Katie pouts. She's shivering a little, too. I believe her fury frightens even her.

I put my arm around her, and we walk into the house.

TWENTY-EIGHT

Jennie

I wake to the noise of the porch swing creaking. There's no movement in the house, so I can hear Ezra and the girls breathing. Anna May sleeps beside me, making that soft kitten purr sound from her nose, her thumb still in her half-open mouth. I slip out of bed, pausing at the door to look at them. It's so strange to see Ezra sleeping between my sisters with his arm around Anna and his head resting on Katie. This is the first time he's slept in our bed since he was three or four.

The night's clear. Moonlight spills through our window, bends across the floor and up the wall. I walk across its path. Cold creeps through the wood under my bare feet. There's light coming from the kitchen.

I peek out the window seeing Mama on the porch wrapped in Mamaw May's thick gray shawl. She hums soft to herself curling her long hair around her fingers. She only wears her hair down at night after a bath and just before bed. I remember being little and seeing it, just as it is now, long and braided, laying across her shoulder, only a few hairs escaping framing her big brown doe eyes and high eyebrows. Mama's still beautiful. She's looking at her hands and rubbing them together. She stops and stares straight ahead at nothing in particular. When she hears me coming out on to the porch she doesn't turn to me. She must be thinking of Daddy. I don't know what to do, so I stand beside her.

She just keeps looking off into the blackness. "Mama," I start. I want to tell her it's too cold to be out so late. She ought to come inside and have something to eat. She ought not worry. We'll take care of her. Instead, I stroke her hair. After a few moments she sighs and concentrates again on her knuckles. I rest my hand on her shoulder. "Mama."

She stops swinging and pats my hand, but still doesn't look at me.

I go back inside and stand in the kitchen, watching her from the window and see her in the same position. I can't bring her back from this. I can't change anything or do anything. I suddenly been feeling as young as Anna.

I know we'll have to move soon. Ezra can't make enough scrip to feed us all. And there's nothing I can do to help him. Nothing I can do to help Mama.

I just won't think anymore tonight. I crawl back into bed and fall into sleep again listening to the sound of the swing.

TWENTY-NINE

Jennie

I stand in line at the company store with Anna on my hip.

Here comes Mr. Hernandez's daughter Maria. She has a real pretty little dark-skinned girl with her. The little girl is holding hands with a boy a little bigger than she is. She seems to be sucking her thumb. I don't know if she's friendly with whites, so I don't say anything. She gets in line behind me, and Anna says, "Hello."

"Hola." The woman replies.

I turn around. "I'm sorry. She talks to everybody." I notice the little girl's eyes first. They're the color of coal and seem to shine or look like she's about to cry. Then I see the woman's eyes are just as dark. "I'm Jennie, and this is my sister Anna May. We live across the alley from y'all. I seen you moving in the other day."

The woman looks down a little shyly, then back up at me. She smiles. "I'm Maria. This my sister Angelina, my brother Antonio. We're just moving here to be . . . for it . . . father to be working at the mine. I no speak the English yet good. Please to forgive."

"No, no I don't mind. I think you speak English just fine." I can tell she doesn't want me to ask her any more. "It's nice meeting y'all." I turn back around.

Her skin is like sandstone or the sky in the morning before a storm. Like so many of the Mexican and Italian women I've seen, she looks like she belongs some-where beautiful. I think about the house I know she lives in, how it's exactly like mine, and all the others the company manufactures. Her long black hair and bronze skin just don't match with the white paint peeling from the boards of her house or the God-awful green shingles falling down from her roof all over the place, littering her small yard. The mountains behind our houses, though, she matches those. I've seen Mrs. Mendez sitting under a tree in the fall. That background matched her. It was something colorful like the rainbows I see in her skin. Lord, those colors. It seems like it gives them the right to sing, as if everybody ought to sit down and listen just because. How I wish I wasn't plain with my pasty white skin and dark brown hair. I have it in plaits today, but it doesn't look like Maria's plaits, neat and perfect. If we were flowers, I'd be a simple dandelion, yellow and forgotten and stepped on, or turning white and fragile, being blown about to make other people's wishes come true, or for their simple, short-lived amusement. But Maria, she'd be a giant yellow peace rose, tinted with pink and white and so fat it fills up both your hands. She'd be the kind that smells so sweet you can catch the scent on the wind for miles, the kind of scent that sticks in your hair for the whole day after you pick so many of them. She would be the kind of flower too pretty to pluck. Instead, you'd admire it and watch it grow, support it with sticks so it could climb up high above your head.

Mama had one of them, but it died. Uncle Cletis got it for her somehow, and it was in our front yard. I don't know where he found it. I'd love to have another one of those rose bushes.

The mountains that crowd us down in this valley are beautiful even though they suffocate us. Seems like sometimes they suck the air right out from the valley and don't leave anything down here for us but coal dust flying, day and night, from the nearby tipple in the center of our camp. Yeah, they breathe up all our good air. But other times the wind blows and we can watch the light and dark greens entangle in what must be some kind of rain dance. Then there's autumn. Another thing I love and hate about these mountains is sour-sweet autumn. They cry, letting leaf-shaped tears gather on the ground, first in vibrant red and shocking yellow, then finally brown, crispy and dead. But I ain't no tree in a mountain shaking my hair in summer or crying leaf tears in autumn, and I ain't no peace rose singing its smell into the cold wind that escapes the holler in spring. Feels like I'm forgotten underneath the coal dust that snows on my face all year.

THIRTY

Ezra

Every day, I pass the armed guards as I enter the drift and start my way down into the mine. Every day I want to join the union more. I shouldn't have to be guarded by men with guns every time I work. None of us should. There's several new colored miners moved into the colored camp. Already talk about which of 'em is union and which of 'em ain't.

Bill's walking beside me, and a bit to the left of us is Saul Williams, a black man who stands a head taller than all of us. I already know he's union. I heard someone talking about him yesterday when I was at the pool hall. Bill looks around and leans over to me. He whispers, "Everybody says he's the most uppity colored man they seen come through Blue Diamond. Another one of them sharecroppers from Mississippi, they say."

Saul looks at us suspicious like, like maybe he knows we're talking 'bout him, but he says nothing. I wonder what he's thinking.

We walk a few hundred yards in silence, and the ceiling of the cave starts to get lower. We crouch down a bit continuing to walk toward the face of the mine. Today like every day I pray I come out alive at the end of my shift. I pray I don't set my timber wrong and have a slate fall on me. I pray I don't get crushed up by a coal car. Pray I don't get blowed up. I think of what Isaac told me about the rats. When I was about twelve and started working, Isaac told me 'bout 'em. The idea of it scared me more than the idea of going deep into the dark to work. He always said if I seen rats running to follow 'cause they head for the outside when something's about to happen—they're always first to know.

Several of us are walking, but no one's speaking. My carbide light's the only thing I can see in here now. Air's getting a little cooler. The silence is uncomfortable. I hear water dripping. "My brother Isaac and Daddy was killed in that flood," I say. "Makes me want to see things change 'round here."

The ceiling gets a little lower and we all crouch a little more.

Saul asks, "What kind a change you talkin' 'bout?"

His friend Jackson gives a look to him as if to say be careful. Jackson's a colored boy I known my whole life, but ever since all these colored got hired at our mine, he's been acting like he hardly knows me.

"I'll tell you how things go here," Saul says. "You do your work and don't stick your nose where it don't belong, and. . . . Talk quiet."

"Listen, Ezra" Bill says. "We got to start crawlin' down in this hole, see. Let's do that and not talk 'bout nothin' else. You wait until I come by your house tonight and get you, you understand?"

I nod.

I bend down and begin to crawl behind Bill. The space is getting tight now. As I crawl, I feel the cold seeping through my pit pants, making my knees ache. I just want to get in my room and get to working. Hope I ain't forgot nothing. Got my auger, shovel, dust shovel, my powder. Got to hurry. My time don't start until I get to the face.

THIRTY-ONE

Anna May

Ezra's friend Bill and Uncle Cletis help us move our things out to the wagon. I want to ride in the back. Bill comes and moves our rocking chair in the back, and I want to sit in it, but Jennie says I'd fall out on my head. So, I sit up front with Bill instead of riding in the back, but that's fine by me. I told Jennie I'm gonna marry Bill when I grow up. She says he's too old. I don't mind! He's got nice dark hair and pretty blue eyes, and I like how he don't chew or smoke because then when he tells me jokes and laughs in my face, his breath don't stink like a lot of other men's. He's real funny, too. He tells me stories 'bout his dogs and 'bout growing up on a farm how my family did before I was borned. That was a real long time ago. We moving our things to Mamaw May's house, and we gonna let folks stay with us. We gonna have a boarding house and have all kinds of people 'round all time. Katie ain't real happy. She says she don't want no foreigners staying with us how they did when Mamaw used to have boarders. But I like foreigners. I sure do. Mr. Mendez used to live with Mamaw May and when he did he made me a rocking horse out of a tree Mamaw asked him to cut down in the yard. I liked it real well.

I look up at Bill and smile real big. He smiles, too. I don't think he'll be too old to marry when I grow up. I like him. And I bet he could build me things, too.

I wrap my arm 'round his arm.

THIRTY-TWO

Nandor

Dearest Family,
I am in the town they are calling Caney Branch.
I am moving to a boarder house in a valley. I begin
work tomorrow in the mine, and they have allowed me to
draw the money called the scrip before I am even working
yet. I am paying for the rent with this until I am mak-
ing more pay. I am never seen so many trees in my life,
my family! It is being beautiful here and, in the night, I
am seeing all the stars in the sky. Here there are many
farmers and people who grow things to sell how you and
Papa do. I am hoping the vineyards are healthy and
well for you and Papa.
I miss you, all my brothers and sisters. I love you, my
dearest family, and may God Bless you. I pray you to be
with me soon. I am writing you again soon.

Yours,
Nandi
Sept. 28, 1918

THIRTY-THREE

Katie

I sit at the kitchen table chopping ramps and soaking a rag in some camphor to help Mama breathe. Jennie sits next to me chopping potatoes for supper. The sharp smell of the ramps makes my eyes water up. Mama's chest been hurting her something awful, and she coughs so hard. This will help. Mama's sick. This house don't feel right without Mamaw in it, and now we're starting to take in boarders.

I hate everything right now.

"Jennie," I say. "I know we got to have boarders to get by, but we ain't gonna take in just anybody, are we? I mean, foreigners and coloreds, too?"

"You like Mr. and Mrs. Mendez, right?" Jennie asks.

"But Mr. Mendez ain't no foreigner, Jennie." I roll my eyes.

"Katie, yes he is."

"Bull Hell. He is not. He don't—I don't know—he don't smell funny, and he ain't stupid," I say.

Jennie looks at me like I said something wrong. "He's from Mexico, Katie. He *is* a foreigner. Just because you've known him since you was little doesn't mean he ain't foreign. And stop saying Bull Hell before Mama hears you. You sound like a boy."

Mama limps into the room.

I keep chopping. Got to heat up these ramps. Find a pot to do that with. Get the camphor and ramp smell off my hands first. Lord, it smells.

Mama coughs. She says, "Jennie, what you been

teaching your little sister? I don't want to hear any more about anybody being stupid or smelling. I didn't raise you two that way."

"Mama," Jennie says. "I was telling her Mr. Mendez is a foreigner but that there ain't

nothing bad about being a foreigner. Why do you always have to blame me when Katie thinks something silly?"

I don't think nothing silly no more than Jennie does. "Mama, she didn't tell me anything. I say what I think about foreigners and coloreds, and that's just what I think. Now, let's get you back in bed. I'll put this on your chest. Draw that cold right out."

She nods weakly. A few weeks ago Mama wouldn't a went on for half an hour about something like this. She's just so wore out. I take her elbow and walk with her to the back of the house. I hear her rattle when she coughs. She holds my elbow tight. Mama breathes in deep. "Katie," she says, "we're gonna board whoever we have to and we'll take in some washings. Ezra don't make enough. We got to do what we have to. It won't be so bad, baby. You'll see."

"Mama, Ezra been talking about union." I say. "All this union junk. It all just sounds like trouble to me."

"You're worrying too much, Katie," Mama says.

They went on strike at Amherst, and I hear all them people living in tents now. People got shot, too. Union didn't bring them nothing but trouble. It ain't gonna bring us anything different.

She steadies herself, leaning on my shoulder as she crawls into bed. When she coughs, she sounds like Mamaw May did. I shiver.

THIRTY-FOUR

Jennie

I close my eyes and lean back in the rocking chair on the front porch. It's almost warm enough out here to sit without this quilt. It has little holes in it, and the half cold, half warm air sneaks through them. Mamaw May's quilts are the strongest damn things. Think I've had this since I was four or five. I like having something she made to wrap around me.

The sun comes onto the porch and warms up my legs, my face. The air always looks yellow when fall is close or in summer. I can tell by the way the air smells more like ice some days and mud on others that fall is disappearing into winter.

Anna comes flying out the front door. "Jennie, read me my book!" she says.

"Lordy mercy, ain't you tired of this story yet?" I say. I've read this book a hundred times at least." She scrunches up her nose at me. "Well, come sit up here with me. It's a little chilly."

She smiles, claps a few times and jumps up in my lap. She accidentally digs her knee right in my stomach when she climbs up. Anna takes the book and flips through it. She doesn't seem too concerned about knocking the wind out of me.

"Watch out now, bony butt," I say, chuckling. I wrap my quilt snugly around us both. "This is the story of CinderAnna, remember? Remember!"

"How come we don't have books like this at school, Jennie?"

I don't really know why we don't have more books—better books. Our books are always about manners and spelling instead of stories. They sneak in there things that tell us girls how to sit and how to act and why it's good to pray every night. While I ain't got a problem with praying, I ain't sure how I feel about the rest of it. "I don't know. Maybe they just don't really know where to get this kind of book from. You reckon?"

"We're special 'cause we got this book. Ain't nobody around here got a book like this, by God!" She laughs at herself.

I got some books Papaw's sister left him after she died. She was a school teacher. I've read *Romeo and Juliet* a hundred times. When I was little, she read me Shakespeare's poems. I didn't understand them but I loved the sound of the words.

Anna flips through the pages and stops on the page with a picture of Cinderella. She's beautiful, and the Prince instantly falls in love with her. I don't think anyone has ever loved me. I believe if Golden loved me we'd been married a long time ago, even if his family didn't want him to. Will someone fall in love with me someday? It just doesn't seem real for the Prince to love her right then. Will my problems disappear like Cinderella's when I get married? I can't imagine a man really digging his hands down deep into who I am and handling all of it carefully.

"I want to look like her when I get big, Jennie," Anna says.

I brush her hair with my fingers. "Anna, I wouldn't waste too much time worrying about that." I don't know what to tell her about this book, about being a woman, about growing up. I don't know the answers myself. But I hope she never stacks her dreams around beauty. What kind of dreams are those? If your dreams are just pretty pictures, they wrinkle, disappear or fade to gray as time moves over them like so many waves. And no one can stop time. No one's ever beautiful forever. Not even Maria. Not even peace roses or trees in summer.

I hear a motorcar coming in the distance. It approaches and stops right at our gate. The passenger gets out and rummages in the back seat looking for something. I notice the stranger's black hair right away. He's a strong man with big arms and hands, but I can tell from here he isn't especially tall. He stands very straight. He looks up and sees us gawking at him. He pulls out a suitcase from the back seat of the motorcar, and now he's staring at us, standing there holding his suitcase. I don't care. I just keep watching him. He's unusual looking. Italian? I can't figure out if I think he's handsome or not. The motorcar pulls away and leaves the stranger with his brown suitcase in the alley.

"Bet anything he's a foreigner," I say.

Anna giggles. "He's a pretty fella, ain't he, Jennie?" This child knows my every thought before I say a word.

I keep watching him. He has a young, strong face. His face won't let me move or speak. Finally, he gives a stifled smile and a wave of the same kind. He seems nervous. He comes into our yard.

Anna watches him and me. Then she laughs again, wiggling in my lap.

"Hush, Anna." I know the expression on my face must be funny. I feel like I know him from somewhere.

Like we share some sort of knowledge, like there's a thin wire connecting us to each other. I think we will be some kind of friends. I can sense this. Anna drops the book on the porch and calls for me to get it. I grab hold of her with one arm and lean forward to reach it. I watch him as he walks up our porch steps. I must not slip. But I'm slipping. Don't slip!

THUD! I drop Anna, almost falling on her.

I realize he's smiling, maybe laughing.

"Ugh, dropped me right on my head, Jennie!"

He stretches out his long hand.

"My name is Nandor. I help you." He pulls me to my feet.

I take his suitcase. "Come on in. I'm Jennie. This is my little sister, Anna May."

She grabs his fingers and tugs. "I am not. I'm Little Bird," she says.

"Little Bird," he repeats, smiling. She likes him right away and smiles a wide toothy grin back, her eyes shining at him like I feel like mine must be.

We walk inside. Already it's strange living in Mamaw's old house. Just don't feel right without her here. I take a key from the wall behind the desk.

"It's fifteen dollars a month rent. Now, we provide supper but men buy what they want for their lunch. We get up and pack the buckets in the morning for you. If you need anything else, you can go on down to the company store and ask them for some scrip to buy you some things. That'll come out of your first pay. Any you take out after is done the same way. I'd try not to take out too much if I were you. You'll go six months without a paycheck if you ain't careful." I'm talking too much.

Anna starts dragging his suitcase down the hall. It's bigger than her. She drops it.

"I'll get that, Anna. Where you from, Mister Nandor?" I scoop Anna off the stairs as we walk up.

"Please to call me Nandi. Budapest, Hungary. I meet nice man from the mine when I come from the ship. He take much of us to work in the mine here. I am having many brothers and sisters. I come here to make it ready for them to come."

He's one of the first men to really talk to me other than my brothers, and even they didn't talk to me very much. I bet we are gonna be friends. "You play cards?" I say. I show him to his room, hand him the key. "Mama hates it when us girls play, but it's great fun. You come on down in a bit, and we'll play a few hands. Gotta watch for that cat-eyed sister of mine, Katie. She'll take the shirt off your back if you're a gambling man."

THIRTY-FIVE

Ezra

Thank God it's time to get home. We walk out the mouth of the mine, and it's dark. Never get out before dark. Mr. Hernandez comes out just behind me, Saul and Nandi, our new boarder.

The guard looks at Mr. Hernandez and nods to a second guard. They stop Mr. Hernandez. "Who was you back there talking to?" the first guard asks him.

Mr. Hernandez shrugs.

What should I do? Anything? Most of the men done left. All save us few. Saul and Jackson comes out, step back when they see the guards. We all watch.

"We do something, I am thinking?" Nandi says.

"I don't know," I say.

Maybe they just hassling him. Maybe it won't get worse. Mr. Hernandez put his hands out like he's trying to explain something and one of the guards pushes him. I can tell a fight 'bout to happen.

I go over. I help him to his feet. He's out of breath. "You got no right," I say.

"You Isaac's brother, ain't you?" the first guard asks. "Must be dumb as he was." He looks at his partner, laughing. He slams the rifle into my stomach.

I bend over, mouth watering. I might throw up. I stare at his shoes. See his buddy being dragged away by Saul and Jackson. Nandi stands to the side looking on. Inside, I'm shaking but I won't shake for him to see, no.

I feel the sweat balling up in my hands and warmth running through my face. This pisses me off more. I ram into him. We both slide in the dirt. I pin him to the ground with my knees, throwing my fists into his face again and again. Bastards. For my brother. For all of us. Blood smears across my knuckles, splatters with each punch. I feel the eyes on my body and see the feet—all those men standing around us watching quietly. I say nothing when I stop. I look at the guard's torn face, my swollen knuckles. What next? Shit. Think. I pull at my hair. Feels like something's stuck in my throat.

Saul yells, "Hit him again!" His voice sounds far away.

I stare at the rifle that lays beside his outstretched, limp arm. He moves his head, mumbles, but doesn't try to get up. I could shoot him right now. This is what he gets for all the days he harassed us, all the miners he beat up. There's something in the guard's hat. I pick it up off the dirt. I pull out a tattered picture of him with a woman and four children. "Oh, God." This makes me not want to do this, but I'll hang for sure if he lives, and I got a family, too. I sling the hat. The second guard is sprawled nearby in the dirt, also bloody. I hadn't noticed they beat him. I lift the rifle, aim. My finger shakes. I see his face at the end of the barrel.

Saul snatches the rifle from me. No one has a voice. No one can move. It's like we're in a dream. He fires into the guard, then the other. Blood bubbles from his mouth. I feel like my stomach's a bucket of water, and the bottom just fell out of it. He drops the rifle. "We need to have a meeting tonight," Saul says, patting my back.

A pain shoots through my hand. I realize my knuckles are split wide open on my right hand. They all start toward home except me and Nandi. We just stand still a moment. He looks at me with big eyes. He looks like he seen a ghost. I look up at the dark clouds and black ones overlapping, moving above us. We're so small compared to them and the shadowy mountains. I look again at the dead guards.

"We got to get gone," I say.

Nandi nods.

I catch up with the others.

Nandi lags behind me.

I must got more Daddy and Katie in me than I knew. Maybe even some Uncle Cletis seeing as how damn stupid that was. Ain't no way we'll get away with this.

"I don't know 'bout y'all boys, but I call for a strike," Saul says. "The mine guards got to go."

I nod.

The others do, too.

Nandi stands next to me now. He says nothing, just looks at us all uneasily then begins the walk home before the rest of us move.

Katie

Ezra walks in the kitchen with a colored, Saul Williams, and our new boarder, Nandor. All three of 'em dirty with coal head to toe. He ought not to have coloreds here. Farmers up and down this holler ain't too crazy 'bout coloreds. First thing that gets stole, they'll be up here banging on our door seeing 'bout lynching Saul. They won't care if he done it or not. I'll wait until later to say something to Ezra about it.

Ezra lays his metal lunch bucket on the table. I notice his knuckles are bloody. "Katie," he says, "I brought somebody I was wanting y'all to meet."

"Ezra, what in God's name happened to your hands?" I say.

He don't answer. Something's going on.

Nandi looks nervous or something. Jennie said she thinks he's handsome. Lord, that girl's strange. He just looks like a foreigner to me. I don't know why Jennie thinks he's handsome. His skin too light and his hair too dark. Plus, he has a strange shaped mouth, sort of full like a woman's. He got some weird way he walks too, like he ain't sure which way he's going. I admit he's handsome for a foreigner anyhow, but only for a foreigner. He looks around the room lots, fast like. Oddball for sure. I ain't real comfortable 'round these folks just yet. Mamaw May's foreign friends was almost like family. Grew up with them. These here folks I don't know, and they seem odd to me.

Jennie and that foreigner keep glancing at each other.

Good God. "Anybody seen Little Bird?" Jennie says. "She needs to get in here for supper."

Well, speak of the devil and here she come. Anna runs in the room, looks up at Nandi, scratches her head, then runs out the front door. "I forgot my doll at Camille's! Be back!" she hollers. Front door slams. God, my baby sister spending all her time at the colored camp and my big sister acting like she struck on a damn wop, or whatever in hell Nandi is.

"Saul, you're staying for supper," Ezra says.

Good God, Ezra. We can't feed the whole of Blue Diamond. I swear we give away more food than we ever eat.

"Well," I say. "I'll fetch some water for y'all to wash up. Y'all just gonna have to take your turn using the same water. My back's a hurting me. I ain't going out and getting more."

Jennie looks at me. "Katie, you're rude," she whispers.

"So," I reply. I walk outside to the well.

THIRY-SEVEN

Jennie

This whole day lagged. Not a person came to visit. Not a letter arrived. The whole place is clean, as clean as an old worn out house could be, anyhow. Did all the washing today. Spent an hour trying to get the tats out of Anna's hair. I sure wish that child would learn to use a comb. Can't do a thing with her. "Katie," I say, "you ought not to let Anna sneak them shells in the camp without telling me. I don't care if it was to help the union. I can't believe y'all let her deliver them to that horse's ass, Uncle Cletis, and at the pool hall no less. The pool hall, Katie! Full a drunks and gamblers."

"Calm down," Katie says, rolling her eyes. "All she did was sneak a pillowcase of shells in the camp. They didn't get her drunk and send her off to fornicate with the devil!"

I just sigh. "Forget it," I say. I got to get some coal. Ezra forgot. It's damn cold in here. I start to get up, and the door opens. A colored woman comes in, holding two suitcases. This woman is the most regal woman I ever did see, white or colored. She carries herself how Mama tried to get us girls to when we was little. We never did have that thing though, that rhythm in our steps and arch to our backs that made us stand tall above everybody else in the room. This woman does. Her black hat has a wide brim that curves and bends just enough to let you see her face, but her eyes are lost under the hat in shadows. One black feather sways on her hat when she walks. That beats all. "I never seen the beat," I say, under my breath.

This woman ain't no woman. She's a lady, like the kind I read about. Her skin's what I know people call "high yellow." Black folks that's got a white mama or daddy. I've seen dark women that were pretty, and I've seen high-yellow women pretty, too, but this one is prettier than all of them. Her chin's a little crooked, with a dimple on it. Her face is thin, but her arms and legs are thick with muscle. She's not perfect, but she's real like the dirt or the flowers that spring up from its belly. And this makes her beautiful. Makes you wonder what her voice sounds like. Is it as unusual but smooth like her walk? She seems like a woman to be reckoned with. Her hips match her shoulders as she steps with care, and her arms sway at her sides. She's got grace like an angel must have, with high feathered wings and robes flowing like water around her. She glows. It ain't just because of her eyelashes that point at the tip or her dimpled chin. She has a light around her just because. She seems like she comes from a different world. A big city? A far away country? Born near an ocean or nestled between bosoms of the Rocky Mountains? I can't say either way. Wonder what she's doing somewhere like this?

In this drab boarding house she looks like a solitary gladiolus. Before August's last gladiolus dies, it leans wearing its tender white or purple bonnet surrounded by sagging brown brothers and sisters whose faces hang toward the earth, mourning their own demise. And so it stands out: the last August gladiolus, the last flicker to a fire before it sinks into earth and rises as nothing more but rings of smoke.

"Hello, I'm Ms. Fannie Garrison. A gentleman told me this is the nearest boarding house to Blue Diamond Camp. Do you have a room available?" Her accent is sharply southern, but she speaks real proper like.

Katie looks at me, surprised. She whispers, "I can't believe a colored asking for a room, Jennie." Ms. Garrison's eyebrows move when Katie speaks, as if she hears, and she looks back at the door.

"We got a room," I say. "It's fifteen dollars a month. Upstairs. Want to see it?"

Katie hangs her mouth wide open. She kicks me in the leg from behind the desk. I kick her back hard. "Damn, Jennie," she whispers.

Ms. Garrison unclasps her purse and hands me twenty dollars. Lord, this is the first person we had give us a whole month's rent up front.

"I thank you kindly, Ma'am. I'm Jennie. This is my sister Katie. We got another little sister, Anna May, and a brother, Ezra. My mama's name's Mary. We all live here. You'll meet the other boarders on Sunday. They're all coal miners, and you ain't going to see them until Sunday unless you stay up until four in the morning. What you doing coming to Caney Branch, if you don't mind me asking?"

"Thank you for the hospitality," Ms. Garrison says. "I'm a teacher. I'm here to open a school for the colored children living in the camps."

I hand her the key and tell her it's room three upstairs. She picks up her bags and starts her way up the steps. We watch her the whole time.

Katie snickers. "I never seen a hat so big in my life, Jennie."

"Well, I like it," I say. "I think it makes her look real

important, like she's a mayor's wife or something. And I'll thank you to shut your stupid mouth, Katie." She looks like the women I saw in my dream when I walked down the black road with the white crosses at the end. Those women were white, but I think Ms. Garrison belongs in my dream. She looks like she could walk anywhere, and never trip.

THIRTY-EIGHT

Jennie

Every one of us sits still on the porch, listening. I look up at the dark sky. The wind feels warm between my bare toes. Ezra sits quietly, holding his fiddle in his lap. Saul's quiet, too, and he has put his harmonica in the front pocket of his shirt. Nandi sits on our swing, his guitar resting in his arms, and he picks something slow I've never heard before. He plays for a few minutes, then starts singing in Hungarian. All of us are drawn. We lean in as if we're one body, like Nandi has cast a spell on all of us. Anna sits on the swing next to Nandi, carefully studying his hands as they touch life into strings that appeared soulless before. Now they sing like life's theirs to tell about.

The words mean nothing to me but move with music like honey. All the words run together into long phrases with breaths in between. He looks out, not at any of us—he just looks past us. His black eyes seem to soak up the darkness as if they're pulling down the evening like a shade.

THIRTY-NINE

Jennie

I sit with the washtub between my legs, dragging the shirts up the washboard and pushing them back down into the water. Washing powders sting sore spots on my fingers, skin already rubbed raw from scrubbing the floor yesterday. "Mama seems so worn down," I say. "But what with Ezra worrying her, runnin' around talkin' about the union blowing up mines, I guess it's expected she'd come down sick."

Fannie sits on the sofa next to me, reading. She wears a plum-colored pantsuit with a long gray dress coat she keeps hung next to the door. I've never seen anybody dress like her except in pictures. "Have you sent for a doctor for your mother?" she asks, turning a page.

"How you, pretty lady?" That ain't Fannie's voice. Golden? When'd he get here?

I look up from my washing. "Great balls of fire, Golden. Would you please knock before you come in?" I got my hair all tied up on top of my head in a mess, my sleeves rolled up, a dirty washtub between my thighs with soap running clear down my elbows, and who walks in but Golden, all dressed up in his sheriff's uniform?

Fannie smiles at Golden and quietly puts her bookmark in her book and sets it on the sofa. As she leaves the room, she raises her eyebrows at me and half-smiles like she just caught me doing something I wasn't supposed to be doing.

I blush because somehow I do feel as if I been caught!

Golden knocks on the wood doorframe and smiles the way he always does. "There. I knocked," he says. He has the most sincere smile. The last time I saw him, he looked troubled. Now he's back to his flirting.

Seeing his smile when I can't touch him, this does something to me—like a sweet sip of hot tea burning the edge of my lip. I run fingers through my hair trying to smooth fly-away hairs. I want to hide what my face must be telling him. "Golden," I say, trying to speak steady. "Go find somebody to arrest. Can't you tell I have things to tend to?"

He leans on one hand against the door frame.

I try to sound like I can't stand him. I hate it when I sound like I'm flirting when I talk to him. I don't want him liking me. He needs to go back up on the hillside there where his family lives, all nice and far away from the black coal dust that gets on every damn thing in my house. Gets on everybody's house who ain't lucky enough to be kin to a foreman or an engineer or anybody else of real consequence. I swear, there ought to be a law against making any folk live this way.

"Jennie, darlin'," he says, "I know you just playin' a little spit fire." He comes and pulls a chair from behind the front desk. He turns it around backward, puts it right in front of me and sits down with his arms crossed against the back of the chair. I hate it when he gets this close to me. He stares at me like I should be saying something, and I don't have a damn thing to say or I forget what to say or I just feel something move in the pit of my stomach.

"Oh, well, don't wait for anybody to ask you to sit down," I tell him, feeling myself half smile. That was so stupid. Why did I say that? I sound like I'm flirting. I look right into his blue eyes, and he lets me. I hate those eyes. He's a devil. I don't want to look at him. He always knows how to smile to make every woman in the room look at him. I try not to smile at him. I just grab another shirt, thinking about starting my laundry again but I don't. I try not to believe him when he says anything that means anything, but I smile anyway, and I listen. I don't know why I do this. I must be crazy.

"I know you like me, Jennie, even if you say you can't stand my whole family and wish we'd all move back to South Carolina. You can't fool me. Can't hide a smile when you got dimples like yours, girl."

I hate him and his blue eyes and everything else about him that makes women notice him, the way he walks into a room and lights it on fire. He has that accent from down where men talk as slow as molasses in January and as smooth as butter. Usually I can't tell if I want to kiss him or puke on his boots.

"Listen Jennie, what I come to talk to you 'bout's your boarders. Now I wouldn't tell you this if I didn't care about your family. You got a house full of hunks, even got a colored lady and all livin' under the same roof. That just ain't fittin' for a family of white women to do." He pulls out a block of tobacco from his pocket, flips his knife open and cuts off a piece.

"This is our house, Golden. We can keep whoever we please. My Mamaw never did sell to the company. Nobody can tell us who to keep and who not to keep." I drop the clothes into the washtub, and suds come up and float on the air.

The front door slams. Katie runs in. "Jennie! You ain't gonna believe wh. . . ." She spots Golden and stops in her tracks, puts her hand on her hip and cocks her head to the side. "Why in hell are you always here, Golden? Last time I checked," Katie says, looking at her pretend watch, "which was just now, all the pigs are supposed to be outside, up in the hills running 'round, not sitting in our house trying to speak human." She crosses her arms and waits for him to shoot back. She smiles, pleased with herself.

"Oh, come on now, Katie," Golden says. "You don't hold nothin' against me, do you? Come on now, don't be so mean."

That smile works on every woman alive except my little sister Katie. She just rolls her eyes. Katie won't ever get along with him. He should've gave up years ago. Get them near each other and they run about like a dog after a chicken, Golden almost always the one with the feathers, of course.

"Golden," Katie says. "You ain't got the sense God gave a goat. Jennie, I'm going to the picnic at the church house. Why ain't you cleaned up? Fix your hair. You look like four different kinds a shit." She takes the ribbon out of my hair, runs her fingers through it and runs upstairs.

I holler, "Just be honest, Katie! Don't worry about hurting my feelings or nothing!" I do look like shit. I hate it when Golden sees me looking this way, too. "Golden," I say, "you came by here to ask me to go with you to the picnic, didn't you?" This time I'm smiling. I can't help it. Sometimes I just can't. That feeling he builds in me is high as a kite. Makes me want to believe he's sincere, even though his past would suggest he ain't and more than likely ain't ever going to be.

I wait for his response. I know that's Katie I hear sneaking back down the steps as they creak under someone's weight.

Golden doesn't answer. He just smiles at me, stands up and walks toward the door. "Nah, I don't think I'm goin' to the picnic. Now, I'm talkin' to you, Jennie, these farmers around here are funny about having a bunch a outsiders movin' up their holler, most specifically coloreds and foreigners. Now I warned you. Just think about it, Jennie. I'll see y'all." He walks toward the door.

I knew he'd pull a stunt like that. He begs me to talk to him, always acts like he's struck on me. The boy gets jealous any time another man comes anywhere near me. But it's always the same thing with him. I ignore him most of the time, because I know he's a lowdown snake in the grass. Then he starts acting like he ain't a snake, like he really does like me. So, when I go to show a little attention to that boy, he goes and reminds me that I ain't quite good enough for him.

"Why'd you ask? Was you wanting to go with me, Jennie? Well, I had no idea of that. You should've told me sooner. I'm sorry about that. Maybe next time?" he says, waving bye, smiling. I just look at him and back down to my wash like he wasn't even there to begin with. He walks out. He ain't never took me no damn where. There ain't no *some other time* with him.

Katie peeks her head around from the stairwell. "I heard what y'all was talking about, Jennie. When are you gonna learn that boy only teases with you? You got to stop liking him. He ain't nobody. Look how he treats you."

I keep washing and lower my head a little, trying not to let on that I care. I feel stupid. He's managed to fool me yet again, even after what an ass he has always been.

She walks over. "Come get cleaned up so we can go. There's plenty of men that would love to talk to somebody as pretty and smart as you," she says, lifting my chin.

"Yeah, I know, Katie. I know," I say. Somehow Golden Motley always seems to know how to make me feel like there ain't a thing pretty about me.

FORTY

Jennie

I take the clothespin out of my mouth and pin it on the line. I take one from my apron and I put it in my mouth. I fold the sheet over the line. The water drips from the fabric and runs in cold, thin paths down my fingers and arms. The wind cuts my skin, makes the water feel like razors scraping against my knuckles. I hate hanging clothes when it's chilly out. Nandi holds my basket for me and just quietly watches me hang each sheet.

"Jennie!" Anna hollers, running into the backyard, "I found somebody that'll take me with 'em to the picnic today. Mama said if I found somebody to go with me I could go, but Golden says if you don't come with us he won't take me neither, and for me to come tell you that." Anna jumps up and down clapping her hands.

I can't believe Golden's nerve. What am I thinking? Of course I can. Nothing he does surprises me. I put another pin in my mouth. I fold the dress over the line. It's too heavy. I'll need extra pins. I put another.

"We're goin' ain't we, Jennie?" Anna smiles big, showing all her teeth.

"Anna. . . ."

She puckers out her bottom lip, and I can't ever say no to her when she does that. I can go and just not talk to him too much, just go, and, well, he did say he was sorry for being how he was being here lately. I don't know. He don't mean nothing, he says. I don't know if

I can stomach that boy all evening long.

"You go get cleaned up then, and I'll come in here in a little bit."

Anna hops around, smiling. "Yea! I love you, Jennie!" She starts running inside.

"Little Bird!" I holler after her, "You're going in a dress, you hear? Katie's finishin' your new one up, and you're wearing it!"

Nandi laughs, still standing there silent, patiently holding my clothes basket.

"A little girl running around in pants all the time. You believe that?" I say. "People would think she was a boy if she didn't have that long hair."

But what about Golden? Lord have mercy, am I ever gonna get away from that boy? What am I going to wear? My dress is dirty. It ain't like I have a lot of clothes. Damn stupid Motley girls will probably show up looking like queens as usual. It'll take me all day to get cleaned up after all the housework I did today. At least Anna will look nice in the dress Katie has been making her. My hair looks like a rat's nest.

I take the basket from Nandi and start in the house. And I realize. . . .

Nandi.

I wonder if he'd like to go. Well, it would be a scandal. But that sure would be fun.

I'll tell Anna Nandi will be our chaperone. She won't care as long as she gets to go.

FORTY-ONE

Katie

I can't get this damn dress just right. Anna don't like dresses all that much anyhow. Can't hardly get her out of them overalls she runs 'round in. Jennie always says *A little girl in overalls! I never seen the beat!* Hell, I say if she likes wearing pants we ought to leave her alone. I prick my finger with my needle. "I can't finish a dress without poking myself a thousand times! Ah, bull Hell," I say.

"Katie, don't curse," Mama says.

Anna runs in.

"Stand here, Little Bird," I say, yanking her over to me. I hold the dress up to her but she giggles and dances around. "Hold still! Let me see about this hem. Gal darn it, come here!"

"Let go! I got to go wash my face. I'm dirty! And I ain't wearin' no dress nohow!" Anna yells, laughing again.

"Lord," Mama says. "What around here ain't dirty?" She laughs.

Jennie steps in from out back, clothes basket balanced on her hip and Nandi behind her. He takes one look at me, and I roll my eyes. He looks uncomfortable and goes upstairs. Good. He makes me uncomfortable, too.

"Child never closes a door" Jennie says. "She acts like she was raised in a pig pen. I didn't know you were back already, Mama."

Jennie plops in the chair across from me. Still has clothespins stuck on her clothes all over. "Mama, you reckon I ought to go to that picnic? I don't know if I should, but Anna wants to go real bad." This has to be about Golden Motley. She thinks way too much about what he thinks and that damn boy don't think anything that makes any sense.

"Jennie," I say, "if you want to go, you ought to go, no matter who's gonna be there or who ain't. Anna wants to go, and if you want to go, y'all go."

Jennie sighs and sits back in her chair with her shoulders slumped. I can tell that didn't do much good.

"Jennie," Mama says in a soft voice. "Don't worry your head 'bout Golden. It ain't gonna mean so much to you when you get older. You're still a young thing. Everything seems bigger than it is."

"I'm not a kid, Mama. I'm eighteen! Past the age to marry. Who cares if it's big or small anyway?" Jennie's so irritated. That boy gets under her skin like nobody else can. I hate this for her. Golden's so damn ignorant.

Mama says, "Golden wouldn't know a good woman if one fell on him, and from what I seen, they do all the time. He's not worth a dime. Why don't you ask somebody to go with you two? Maybe you'll feel better about it then."

Jennie chews at her fingernails. She looks at the floor, then says, "I just ought not to go because Golden's going to be there thinking I'm there just because he is, the skunk. He's so full of himself. Maybe I'll ask Nandi to go with me."

Darn. Prick my finger again.

Anna hollers about being ready to go and for Jennie

to hurry and get herself cleaned up. Jennie sighs. Looks so upset. Driving herself crazy worrying about   that fool.

"You got to think about yourself more, Jennie" Mama says. "You're thinking way too much about Golden. He's a bunch a meanness and, well, he's just young I reckon, but that don't make how he acts right." It's good Mama is saying this to her. She ought to hear these sorts of things.

"I think I'll ask Nandi," Jennie says.

Me and Mama just look at each other with big eyes.

FORTY-TWO

Jennie

I can't believe I asked Nandi to go with me to this thing. I never asked a fella to do something in my life. Katie sits next to me on one of the picnic tables with her arms across her chest and this look on her face like she's not too happy. Nandi sits on my other side.

"Jennie," Katie says, "we're 'bout the only white folks here."

"I thought you wanted to come," I say.

Camille runs up to us, bouncing and grinning. She takes Anna's hand, and they run away to play.

"Be careful!" I say.

"I did want to be here. I just expected, I don't know . . . ," Katie says.

"Well, try to behave yourself," I whisper. I hope she ain't going to be rude to Nandi again. He was awful nice to come with us. He don't hardly know me. It's so awkward. We just watch the crowd and look at each other every now and then and smile. I can't think of a thing to say to him. He must think I'm stupid. People are fanned out all around the churchyard. Some sit at picnic tables, others on quilts. Men have their guitars out. I hear somebody talking about baseball season and how the colored camp up Thistle Bottom gonna beat the whites from Blue Diamond. "I can't believe the weather. It's sure warmed up today, ain't it, Katie?" I say.

Katie sneers at me a little. "I reckon. I'm gonna go get something to drink."

Oh, no. Now here we are sitting by ourselves. I really don't know what to say. I wonder if he knows about me watching him? I try to keep from laughing. I can't believe he seen me upside down with my dress over my head.

I say, "What's your home like, Nandi? Your family?" There, I said something.

Nandi breathes in deep and closes his eyes for a second. What's he doing? He opens his eyes again. "Where I am from, it is being beautiful. People, they are kind. My family is having a vineyard. My Mother sings and my brother, he is a painter. It is my grandfather who teach me to be playing the guitar." He looks around at all the people and back at me. "I am sorry. I am talking much." He can't seem to look in any direction longer than a few seconds. Seems like he's always about to ask a question. When his eyes move across the churchyard, up at the trees then down to my face, he seems to be thinking very carefully about his surroundings. Or, he could be uncomfortable.

"My Mama likes to sing 'round the house. I do, too, but never let nobody but Anna May hear me. My family sings and plays music when we have family reunions, but I never learned to play myself. I'd sure like to learn if you found the time to teach me." I hardly believe I just said that. My God, now I've took to flirting with Nandi. Here I done asked this fella to come some place with me. Can't believe I did that. And now I'm telling him I sing! Who cares if I sing anyhow?

"I like to be hearing you sing," he says.

I blush. Not sure if I'm embarrassed more by what I said or what he replied. Am I falling into his eyes, or is he falling into mine? He's easy to like.

"Well, they havin' a wrestle over there, Nandi," Anna says, running to us and jumping in my lap. "How come you ain't in it?"

"Lord, Little Bird, you about knocked the wind out of me," I say.

"Stand up, Jennie," Anna says, "so we can see." I pick her up and wedge her between my hip and arm, and we peek over the crowd around the men wrestling in the mud and in the grass. I can't believe grown men do this. "Hey, Nandi, won't you go show 'em heathens how it's done?" Anna says, hitting him in the shoulder with a bony little fist.

Just then I notice Golden standing in the circle around the men wrestling. Dust flying all over, and men laughing and hollering. Golden stops carrying on with the rest of him. He puts his hands down to his sides. I can tell he wasn't expecting to see me here. "Anna, let me put you down," I say.

"No, no! Don't sit down. I wanna watch 'em a little longer, Jennie!"

I won't say anything. I'll just try not to pay any mind to Golden. But I know I am. No matter how hard I try, I can't never seem to ignore that fool. He looks at Nandi like he wishes he'd die. Not again,   Golden. Damn you. Stop it. I like Nandi, and you ain't gonna ruin it. He sure is trying to. I feel like screaming inside. Why does Golden act like he doesn't care a thing for me then turn around and act like I'm some kind of territory, like a piece of a land or something?

Nandi knows what's going on

I just laugh a little and bite my lip. Oh, I don't know why he's gawking at you that way. Please don't blame me for it, Nandi.

Nandi smiles a wide, sure smile. He always seems so sure of every expression and word. I love this about him. He touches my face and kisses me. A small, easy kiss.

Anna gasps.

"Hush, Anna," I say. I can't believe he kissed me!

Golden looks like somebody set his house on fire.

I can't hold the laugh in. I cover my mouth with my hand.

"I show them," Nandi says.

He really is looking for trouble. He walks over to the brawl, and two men part to let him in the circle. Then, he points at Golden and says something.

Katie runs over to where we're sitting. "He's gonna whip Golden, Jennie," she says, laughing. "I don't know. Maybe this boy ain't so bad!" She winks at me.

I ain't sure who's going to kill who but, the looks of it, they both want to kill each other. Of course, it's just a game, so I reckon they can't hurt each other too bad. Part of me feels flattered, but another part just feels like—I don't know—like they're a couple of dogs, and I'm a bone they're fighting over. There's another part though, that's really tickled when Nandi wraps his arm around Golden's neck and throws him to the ground like a rag doll.

Katie jumps up and down, along with the rest of the onlookers.

"Jennie," Anna says, tugging at my fingers, "I think Mama's right when she says boys are stupid."

"Now I remember why I call you Little Bird. You're too smart for your age," I say, laughing.

Golden struggles back to his feet, and Nandi waves at me. Apparently he's enjoying thrashing Golden.

I laugh, waving back. First man ever stood up to Golden instead of running straight away. I bet my cheeks are red.

FORTY-THREE

Jennie

"Katie, go stay in the front room," I say, leading her downstairs.

Katie pouts. "Jennie," she says. "I know y'all making something for me, why don't you just let me see what it is?"

I don't answer her. I just point to the front room. She stamps her foot. Her voice is shrill and whiney. "Bull Hell!"

This just makes me want to keep her in suspense longer. I laugh and slap her on her hind end. "Katie, get your ornery self downstairs like I say or you ain't gonna get a thing for your birthday, meanness!"

I trip on my dress going up the narrow stairwell, laughing at her. In the room upstairs, some of my neighbors are sewing in a circle: Elizabeth, her sister Amy, and their cousin Beth Ann. Elizabeth's squatting on a stool, needle in teeth, pinning up the hem of Katie's new dress. I ain't sure what Mamaw May ever used this room for, but it's gonna be our room for quilting and where we wrap our Christmas presents. For now, we hide in here to make Katie a dress for her birthday. I say, "I been buying materials for this thing all year long. A little piece here and another there whenever I could afford it. I even traded some things for some of it." I run the material through my fingers. "This dress'll be just right for Katie now that she's old enough to be courted."

Elizabeth smiles. "You and your sisters are so sweet to each other," she says. "I have to go pretty soon, but I'll stay awhile longer to help you finish up."

There's a rap at the door.

I holler, "Katie, I said get downstairs and leave us be!"

The door opens.

It's Fannie. She pulls a cream-colored lace sash from her pocketbook. "I'm sorry I took so long, but I have it," she says.

"Come on in. Oh, it's beautiful," I say.

Elizabeth and Amy look a little startled at the sight of a colored woman. Farmer's girls. All they ever seen was their family and that farm they live on. It's hard to say what they're thinking seeing Fannie. Beth Ann gets up, knocking over a sewing box. Spools of red, black, white, and green thread roll across the crooked hardwood floor. There's no other sound in the room.

Fannie doesn't seem to notice their reactions or she doesn't care.

Elizabeth gives a halfhearted smile. "I think we ought to get on home," she says. I can't tell if she's scared or offended by Fannie. She takes her hat from the table and just walks out the door. Her sister Amy leaps up too and follows without a word. Beth Ann, too. I believe I should say something, but what? Oh, Lord.

"Jennie," Fannie says, "the holidays are almost here! Is your family having chicken or turkey for Thanksgivings this year? I have a chicken recipe from my grandmother that is just wonderful."

I'm so relieved she changed the subject.

"Well," I say, "I'm going to help Ezra smoke a hog

for Thanksgiving. We did it last year, too. Camille and Little Bird was real upset when Ezra went to slaughter that hog, because one of them's their pet. They call it Pig. They wanted to make sure our Thanksgiving hog was no relation to Pig so we didn't kill one of his kin. Lord, they cried and cried. So, me and Mama drew up a family tree on a piece of paper. We named and mapped out all the pigs we owned so the girls would let us smoke that Godforsaken hog!" Fannie laughs, and I laugh. "I can't believe Katie is turning sixteen," I say. "So many things happened to me the year I was sixteen."

"Something important happens every year of your life," Fannie says. "But sixteen, there's something about that year that changes girl parts of you into a grown up. Sixteen sure was important in my life."

"Tell me about it," I say. "What happened when you were sixteen?"

She looks up and to the right like her eyes are watching her memories come to life on the walls around us. She pins the sash to the waist of the dress and then closes her eyes as she begins to speak. "My Daddy was white. My Mother was half white. They were a scandal in our hometown, and some folks said they shouldn't have been allowed to marry even though Mama didn't really look colored. The summer I turned sixteen was the first time I had the nerve to jump off the railroad trestle. We had built a dam there, and the water was as deep and dark as the mountains around us. I was in the water with Buddy. That wasn't his real name, but that's what we called him. I was sweet on him, and he was sweet on me. But see, Buddy was colored, and my

Daddy didn't like that. He said Mama having colored in her caused enough trouble for our family, and he didn't need us having ugly colored babies with colored people hair making it worse. Folks did terrible things to him for marrying my mother. It made our lives hard. Colored nor white approved of their marriage. So, when our farm neighbors miles up the road found out he had married a half-colored woman, we were run off our farm late one night by the night riders, the Ku Klux Klan. I believe he blamed Mama for the beating we all took that night. I believe a part of him hated himself for loving a woman that was so hard to love. He started fighting with Mama all the time. He drank a bit back then. They yelled, but he never hit her.

"Then she got sick with pneumonia and died. I was sixteen. After her death, he fell apart. He drank so much you could smell the liquor coming up the road before you'd see him. He gambled. He brought home a different white woman every night. We didn't have a thing because of him. What convinced my daddy to quit drinking is what happened one day at the railroad trestle. Like I said, I wasn't allowed to be with Buddy, so he and I would sneak to see each other there. One summer day, Buddy and I floated in the water. We thought we were alone. We didn't realize a group of white kids had come to jump off the trestle and were watching us from above. Buddy pulled a ring from his pocket—where he got it I can't say—and slipped it on my finger. It wasn't anything too fancy—just a silver band—but, to me, it shined like a diamond. He kissed me. That was my first kiss. We walked up onto the bank, and he kissed me again. All we heard was a train rumbling above, and all we saw was light weaving through the trees. I thought for sure I was in love.

"Someone grabbed my arm, and began dragging me up the muddy hillside. It was covered in briar bushes, so my legs were cut up terribly. It was Daddy. He reeked of alcohol. I was sure he'd kill me or Buddy or both of us. He gripped the back of my neck so tight it hurt. He saw my ring and took it. He threw it over the trestle and then backhanded me a good one. Buddy ran home. He didn't even stop to help me. Then Daddy took off his belt and started to beat me. He beat my legs and arms, my back. My brothers and sisters came running, along with my uncles Jack and Reese. They pried the belt from his fist and then beat him. I cried, lying there in too much pain to move. It was my daddy's sister and her daughter Delphia who helped me walk home. Daddy never took another drink, and he never raised a hand to me again. But he never could talk to me after that. He couldn't seem to look me in the eye or tolerate me being in a room with him for too long. So, it was as if I really didn't have a daddy at all, but just a man who kept me clothed and sheltered. That's what happened when I turned sixteen."

She forces a small grin and exhales a long, controlled breath. I sense we don't need to say nothing else. Not just now. We return to our sewing. Muffled voices echo throughout the house, rising and falling in conversation. Every few minutes we hear thumping and banging from Anna and Ezra roughhousing, their hollering punctuated by laughter.

FORTY-FOUR

Anna May

I'm crawlin' underneath the porch to watch all the feet come down the steps, and here comes Jennie hollerin', "Anna! Anna where you at!" She don't know I'm under here.

I found a snail—got a shell big and brown with tiny white spots on it. I touch it on its head, and it hides back down in its shell and won't come out no more. If I squeeze it, I'll hurt it, so I won't squeeze it. I keep it here in my front dress pocket. When I lay on my belly and remember the snail's in my front pocket, I don't think that snail's real happy about me layin' like this, so I get back up. I hope it ain't squished in there. My dress sure is muddy. I'm under the porch though, and the porch is muddy, too.

Jennie's getting' on my nerves hollerin' for me. I ain't supposed to be underneath here, so I will breathe real quiet-like so she can't hear me and I try not to move. It's dark under here, and I can watch feet go down the stairs. Ezra and Jennie sits on the top step, and I hear 'em. I don't see no more feet walkin' down the stairs, just their feet beside each other Ezra tells Jennie somethin' about the union. Jennie says she can't have him getting' hisself killed no way. He says he won't get killed. Jennie says we lucky he ain't been called off to the war

I think Ezra's mad because the Bald-Men-Feltses men come down here yesterday and told Idella Clark— the lady that runs Clark's Market—told her she has to trade with the company store from now on. She can't sell nothin' but company stuff now. Ezra cussed when Idella told him that. Ezra says now Idella's food and things gonna cost too much for anybody to buy. Idella cried 'cause she says she knows she's gonna go out of business now. Idella's colored, so she says it like "bidness." She says "I's a'gwana go outta bidness now, fo' sho'." He sure did like the chew she sold. Now he ain't gonna get no chew no way. And Uncle Cletis will have to quit smokin' cigarettes. And I won't never get no more oranges. Only get those every now and then. Won't get none now. She was the only store besides the company store, and now she's got to close. Company store's oranges costs too much scrip, Mama says.

I hear a man talkin' to Ezra. I see him through the space between the steps. Could see better if Jennie'd move her big ol' clodhoppers out the way. That's a slicky poly-tish-un man talkin' to her and Ezra. I can tell by how his hair is slicked down over his ears. All them are slicky is what Jennie always tells me, 'cause they put that grease in they hair. That slicky-haired man asks for Ezra to vote for him, and Ezra says he ain't votin' for nobody. Ezra says for him to go away. He says he knows his vote don't count no how. Says the company probably owns him like the company owns everybody else around here. When the   slicky-haired man leaves, Jennie says Ezra ought not have said that.

Jennie always says the company buys the slicky-haired men, and that's how come the black dust comes in our windows. It comes in our windows and it sticks to everythin' in the house no matter how much we scrub. I scrub and help Jennie scrub and scrub until my fingers and Jennie's fingers get real red and hurt when we go to take a bath in the tub later. It stings, the water does. The warm water—after Mama gets it hot and pours it in—it burns where we scrubbed and hurt our fingers. Oranges burn my fingers, too. I don't get oranges very often, but when the truck leaves the empty crates out behind the company store, I sometimes dig 'round and find oranges they left behind, and I take 'em home.

When the house shakes from them blastin' up the mountainside and puttin' cracks in our ceiling, Jennie says that's because the slicky-haired men belong to the company, and so they men don't do nothing for us. Ezra always says we got a honest sheriff in Golden Motley, but our local judge's a *piece of shit*. Jennie got mad when I told her Ezra said that. Jennie says I ought not to say *piece of shit*.

I reckon the slicky-haired men go and fix the ceilings at other people's houses, but not in our camp. I don't know why they don't come fix our ceilings for. I think we're awful nice people. Next time a slicky-haired man comes to our door and says if we'll vote for him he'll get us things we want, I'm gonna ask him if he'll come in and fix our ceilings. If he don't, I'm gonna tell him my brother says he's a *piece of shit*, and Jennie can get mad if she wants to.

FORTY-FIVE

Jennie

I can't help it. I want to see what Nandi's doing while everybody's out of the room. I like looking at him. It's definitely not just because he's handsome. He ain't even the most handsome fella in the whole world, but there's something about the expressions on his face that makes him familiar. I always try to read him when I see his face. I never can tell what he's thinking. I want to know what he looks like when he's alone.

I go inside and stand near the coal stove where I can look in the kitchen without him seeing me. I'm not sure what I'll say if he does. I'll think of something.

He's standing at the table by a basin full of water and rolling up his shirt sleeves. He dips his hands in the water. I can't help but stare. It drips from his fingers. He rubs his hands together and splashes water on his face. It drips from his wrists, from his lips and elbows. He sighs heavy and lets his head hang a moment and I wonder what's in that sigh besides his body being tired.

"Jennie, what you doin'?" Anna May startles me. I grab her and pull her behind the stove. I peek over the stove and realize he hadn't heard her. "What you lookin' at? Awe! Are you watchin'. . . ?"

I cup her mouth with my hand. "Hush up, Anna," I whisper.

He starts to peel his shirt over his head.

Anna bites my finger hard.

"Ouch!" I pick her up and run out the door with her. "Get under there, Anna," I say, stuffing her under the front porch. "But you say I ain't supposed to come under here 'cause I'll get dirty, Jennie!"

"Anna, hush! Great balls of fire! Here comes the whole lot of 'em! How you figure we get out from under this porch without them thinking I lost my marbles?"

Anna laughs. I shush her again. Now only the sound of us breathing disturbs the dark. We watch the men's feet as they walk up the porch steps and listen to the boards crack under their weight. Dirt falls into my hair from above. Anna starts to sneeze.

"Oh, you hold it," I say. "Don't you dare sneeze."

She tries to sneeze in her hands and sounds like a small cat getting its tail stepped on. I hear the swing creak as it moves back and forth and see the men through the cracks of the porch floor. They're still talking. Must not have heard the stepped-on cat. "Me and Katie played hide and go seek today, Jennie. I hid under here, and she never did find me. I sit here forever, too. She looked and looked and. . . ."

"Anna, shut up!"

I see Mama walk up the porch steps. The door slams. Nandi comes out. She's speaking to him, but I can't understand what they're saying.

"Why was you watchin' him for, Jennie? You struck on him?" She giggles.

"Anna hush." I tap her in the back of her head. "I'm not struck on anybody."

"Are too."

"Am not."

"Are too!"

"Jennie! Anna, ya'll come and eat!" Mama starts ringing the porch dinner bell.

"Oh, well . . . good. When everybody goes in, we'll come out."

"Not unless I drag you out first!" Ezra hollers, grabbing my leg and pulling me through the wet grass. "You didn't think we heard y'all stupids, did you? You're caught red-handed! I'm taking you to jail!" He holds me upside down and shakes me, laughing.

"Mama! Make him put me down!"

I can see Saul, Jack, Mama and Nandi on the porch—upside down. I struggle to hold my dress close so nobody sees my underclothes.

"Stop it, Ezra! You're gonna break your sister's neck!"

Anna stands beside me laughing, clapping, jumping.

"Here, Ben. Give Jennie a kiss," Anna says, leading our neighbor's goat to my face. It starts trying to eat my hair.

I scream, swatting at it. I reach out to grab it, letting go of my dress. It flies open freely for the whole world to see.

Ezra flips me right side up again.

"I hate you Ben! You stupid goat," I say.

Everyone except me bursts into laughter.

"I don't see what's so damn funny." I pick grass out of my hair wet with spit.

Piece of shit goat.

FORTY-SIX

Anna May

I found my doll at Camille's. Just gettin' back. Who are these men in my kitchen? Oh, I know them. "Mister Nandi, you play the gi-tar, don't ya?" I say.

He smiles. "I do."

"Jennie, can he teach me? Can he teach me, Jennie?" Jennie says yeah.

"Yea!" I holler.

"Anna, don't bother Nandi too much. The man's tired," Ezra says.

Why everybody always think I botherin' everybody? I don't bother people. I want to help Jennie cook. "Jennie, lemme," I say.

"You can't peel no potatoes. You're too little," she says.

Katie comes in from outside with a pail of water.

I ain't too little. Everybody says I'm too little. Well, I can kick Sam's butt for sure. He ain't gonna say that no more. "I whipped Sam today, Saul," I say.

He laughs.

Here come Nandi in with his guitar. Oh goodie! Goodie!

Well, he's dirty, so Jennie makes us sit on the swing outside. "Come wash up when you're done," she says. "And don't touch him, Anna. I mean it. He's covered in coal!"

I go outside. "All right, I won't!" I holler. I slam the screen door. I sit in his lap. "Thank you, Mister Nandi," I say.

He puts my hand on the guitar and puts my other hand on the other part of the guitar and he says for me to hold my fingers and it hurts my fingers.

"Darn! I can't do that," I say.

Nandi laughs at me. He takes my finger with his hand. My hand is turnin' coal-colored like his hands. He tells me to strum the strings, and I try. I put my hand right there and then I say, "You just get off a work, Mr. Nandi? Whew! You sure does stink!" He laughs at me again. My eye's itchin', so I scratch. He puts my hands back, so I try to strum it like he says, with my fingers in the places he says, and it goes ker-CHINK! "That don't sound no good but I done it! You see me do it? Oh, oops, my hands are dirty." My hand got coal on it from his hands. Ew. I strum the guitar real fast like this and I sing, "What the hell on my hand! What the heeeeeeeell on my haaaaaaaaand! I got somethin' on my hand! And it looks like coal but I don't know! What the hell on my haaaaaaand!"

Jennie comes outside. "Anna, what did I tell you about little girls talking like sailors?"

I don't member what she said about that. Oh, wait. Yeah, I do. "You said that if I talk like a sailor you'd send me off so I can be a real sailor if I don't stop talkin' like one," I say.

Nandi laughs and sets me down. I frown.

"Let him alone, now. Katie's 'bout got some water warmed up for these fellas to wash up. Oh, Anna! Look at your dress! It's black! And how did you get it all over your face! I told you not to touch him!" Shoot. It was already black. All my dresses turn black in the camp anyhow.

I sing some more. "What the hell on my faaaaaaaace!"

FORTY-SEVEN

Jennie

"Jennie, are you sweet on Nandi?" Anna says. She giggles.

My mouth drops open. Why is she asking about that? And at this hour! "Whisper, Anna, or you'll wake Katie. Why would you think such a thing?"

Anna giggles again.

Katie shifts beside me but doesn't wake.

"If you don't hush . . . aw, just go to sleep."

Anna laughs some more, then whispers, "He's a handsome fella. Night, Jennie."

I roll over and close my eyes. Nandi. He *is* handsome, but he's probably ornery like the rest. Now, I'm thinking about the first boy who kissed me. He was handsome, too. He sticks in my head. And I think of Anna singing that ridiculous song she made up. I laugh. I think about Nandi. I drift off to sleep.

I'm ten, and on Mamaw May's porch. Everything has a white glare. I rub my eyes so I can see clearly but they don't clear. The sound of rustling trees and running streams fills the holler. Winter has melted. Waters run wild and mad down the mountain, seeking bigger pathways. Behind Mamaw's, one stream dives over the rocks, stretching itself silvery and smooth between the grassy mountain and the creek below. It slithers like a snake. This creek always swells with water and debris and roars after a big rain. I look at the sky.

It's about to rain. I ask, "Is it June, Mamaw?"

Mamaw pets my head. "It's June and I got strawberries need pickin'. Your birthday is next week. Don't you want strawberries for your cake?" She sits next to me, stringing beans into the pot between her legs. She ain't even got to look at what she's doing. Her hands move around each other like a dance or like butterflies. I look into her eyes as she reaches over to caress my cheek with the back of her hand. Then, Mamaw's face fades into the white day.

Next I see Isaac walking up a distant hill. He's smiling, and there's sunlight on his back. Orange all around him. He begins to fade into the orange. The moving grass and high winds seem to blend him with the red sky like a painting. And he disappears as he waves to me.

Now, here's Daddy when he was young and I was Anna's age. We still lived on a farm then. I see his face before he had that hard look from years of coal dust settling into his wrinkles, before the coal dust got through his skin and in his veins, running with his blood and clogging up where his heart's supposed to be. He holds my wrists with his big hands, and I hold his wrists with my little hands as he spins and spins me around in the summer sun. I hear myself laughing—my voice, higher then, squeaked when I laughed like all little girl giggles do. I look up. Trees swirl by and, through the blinding glare of midday sun, I see Daddy smiling.

Then I'm standing under a bright light. Snow's falling on my hair, and the world around me looks blue. My heart's heavy, but I feel as if I could fly. A man stands close to me. I feel his warm breath moving my hair, but I can't see his face.

FORTY-EIGHT

Anna May

I hate school. I hate the schoolhouse. All we do is listen and listen and listen. I hang sideways out my desk and hum.

Now Mrs. Adkins is walking back here. "Anna, honey, please don't hang out your desk like that," she says. Oh, if I didn't think I'd get in trouble I'd probably say somethin' back. I don't know what, but I'd sure say somethin'. I like her hair. It curls 'round her face like big letter *C*s on the sides of her head. Jennie was proud I seen letters in somebody's hair. Jennie says I use my imagination. She says I'm smart.

I want to go home. I want to go home and get Nandi to teach me some more guitar.

I seen that possum again on our porch last night. He's uglier than a mud fence, but he's cute 'cause he hisses like a cat. I'm gonna feed him again tonight, even if Mama says for me not to. I like possums long as they don't get too close to me. They fur feel nasty and prickly like a big ol' rat or somethin'. I'm gonna name him Fred the possum. He got pointy teeth, and he sure do stink 'bout like Pig does, only he ain't wet a lot like Pig. Pig roll in every mud hole from here to the county line. Dirty ol' Pig.

"Jennie, hey Jennie. You wanna go help me try to catch Fred tonight? We can put him in a cage and maybe feed him carrots."

Jennie laughs at me. "Who's Fred?"

"I named that possum Fred."

Mrs. Adkins looks at me all mean and points her finger, so I hush up. She starts handin' out papers. I hope it ain't no homework. I ain't doin' no homework. I do like Katie does and stay home when we get homework most times. "I want to see you after class, Jennie," she says when she walks by our row.

"Ooh, what's Jennie done?" I ask Katie.

Katie ignores me.

Mrs. Adkins got to have her all confused with somebody else. My sister don't never do nothin' wrong. Well, not *that* sister anyhow.

So, everybody leave but me and my sisters.

Mrs. Adkins says, "Jennie, your poem is very good. Everythin' you turned in so far has been excellent work. I'd really like to talk to you about college."

Katie looks surprised and Jennie looks at us like she real surprised, too. Jennie says, "I want to go, but I got to ask my Mama first. I don't know what she'd say about that. Maybe you could tell her for me."

"I'm not ready to talk to your mother about it just yet. How 'bout you come to my house this evenin' and have supper with my family? I'll come to your house another time and talk to your mother, after I hear what you got to say 'bout it, all right?"

Jennie smiles and shakes her head up and down.

We walk outside and start home.

Katie says it's cold and wants to carry me so we'll stay warmer.

I hold my arms out.

"You like a load of bricks, Little Bird. Before long you be too big for me to pick you up at all," Katie says. She starts ticklin' me.

I laugh and wiggle. "You're gonna drop me on my head!"

FORTY-NINE

Jennie

For no particular reason, Fannie and me walk down the holler a little ways at dusk. We should turn around before we get to any houses. We'll turn back at the crossroads. Don't want to run into the wrong kind of white folks. Mountains hug the path on each side. The hard frozen mud rises and sinks in places like waves. Silvery rocks seem to blink in the moonlight. The snowy mountainside wears boulders like diamonds along the valley—jagged, and kissed with ice. The air smells of frosted grass and snow. A week ago it felt like April. Now, flowers sag. Sheer bruise-colored shadows melt in cracks between rocks, and dead bushes look like faces in the dark. I hear my breathing, and when the wind blows, the rattling sound of trees shivering snow from their branches. "What's the most beautiful thing you ever saw, Fannie?"

"That's a pretty good question. Let me think." She's quiet a moment. "I try to see beauty all the time, so I can't pick just one thing. Beauty is everywhere. Some beauty's just easier to look at than other kinds."

"What do you mean other kinds?"

"There's the kind of beauty easy to see. Then, there's beauty living in dark places, like in death. Some people might say there's nothing beautiful about death, but a poet might say that while a dying man sleeps, death reaches into his chest, stopping the clock gently with the tap of a finger. Then, there's no more pain or suffering. Just peace. That's how death can be beautiful."

She goes on to say she thinks fighting and anger can be beautiful, too. Mother Jones is beautiful, she says, the little woman who has made her life about fighting for miners' rights. "You have to fight for yourself and others, too," Fannie says. "That the woman's message. All of us have to fight injustice, some of us in smaller ways than others."

Fannie's wise. But wise is too common a word to describe her. When we met, that feathered hat she wore so casually dazzled me. Now, it seems like an understatement, because she glows quietly as sure as snow shines at night.

Fannie has told me stories about her life and about her family. Her grandmother was a slave whose master got her pregnant. She gave birth to Olivia, Fannie's mama. Fannie described the farm she grew up on, and when she did I felt as if I'd been there all along. I could almost smell the pigs and mimosa trees in her yard and feel the wet heat of southern summer. I could hear her crying when her sisters drowned trying to save their brother from the river. I could also see the look on her face when she opened up that letter saying she had been accepted to the big university for coloreds in the city. Fannie has told me so many stories, and she makes them real to me. No matter how dreadful a memory, she pulls beauty from it like plucking a chestnut from its prickly husk.

She has a small scar on her face. I always wonder what that's from. "Where you get that scar, if you don't mind me asking?"

"I got that from a fall." She doesn't say more but I

press her.

"Well," she says, "I used to help my Daddy pick peaches, vegetables and things. We'd take them to town and sell them. You don't see that so much anymore, not like we did when I was younger."

We arrive at the crossroads and stop. I lace up my boot.

"One of my favorite things to do when I was a girl was ride in the wagon when Daddy drove it into town to sell peaches. What we didn't sell, we'd take and give away. Daddy would holler and all the kids from nearby houses would run out to get a peach or two for themselves or their families. Many of the kids wouldn't have much to eat, so it was a real treat when we'd ride round giving away what we had left. On the way to town I'd lie in back. Daddy made me quit when I turned ten because I was too big and tore up all the peaches. Before then, I'd lie there surrounded by bright gorgeous peaches. I'd look up at how the sun stretched when I squinted my eyes. One day, there were a few kids getting out to the wagon late, but Daddy had already started back toward home. I hollered for him to stop. They were behind us, running. He must not have heard me, because he didn't stop. I thought I would get an armful of peaches and throw some to those poor kids. So, I cradled as many as I could in my dress. I had my foot on the side of the wagon, and just as I threw the first one, I lost my balance and fell out. I landed face first. Blood was all over my dress. I broke my wrist. While I was at home getting well, those kids came to visit. They brought me violets. One of them said he'd have liked to write me a nice note, but none of them could read. They were all farmer's kids, and they wouldn't go to school. They'd stay home to work. But I was lucky. My mama taught me. So, I told the children I'd teach them, and that's how I became a teacher, and also how I got this scar."

Fannie's life is so full of colors. I love her stories.

When we reach the house, already I know something is wrong. Katie comes running out the front door. "Jennie, Mama's real sick." I step around two long, thorny switches laid together in a cross just in front of our door. I thought that was just a rumor. No, the Klan wouldn't. . . . Katie grabs my elbow and pulls me close to her. "What are we gonna do? We got the Klan after us now. We got to get these coloreds outta here. You can't be running around with Nandi no more neither," she whispers. Fannie goes inside, and Katie eyes her sharply.

"Stop treating Fannie like that," I say, pulling my elbow free from her hand. "Probably ain't even the Klan that laid them switches. It's probably Ezra running around with Saul and his buddies got some stupid white folks mad. We'll talk about it later. I'm checking on Mama." I go inside.

Mama's in the kitchen, leaned on a chair, half bent over coughing, blood dripping from her chin.

I feel as if I'm a little girl again, seeing my Mama in this shape. Hearing the noises she's making hurts me. I can't do nothing to help her. I know she'll die soon. I'm motionless and feel as if I'm in a dream of a dream of a dream. "Consumption," I say, and feel dizzy.

FIFTY

Katie

Half asleep. What's that banging noise? I ain't going to school today. I know that's probably Jennie on the porch banging just so I'll get out of bed, and then she can say I might as well go since I'm up. I hate it when she does that.

I hear the banging again. "Stop banging, Jennie! I'm coming!" I holler. I lay here a minute with my eyes open and see Anna May next to me. I must a woke her up.

Anna sits up in the bed and looks out the window. "They's some men on our porch, Katie."

I hear a male voice. "Open up!"

I loaf into the hall. Mama's waking up, too. She scoots into the hallway with her blanket wrapped around her shoulders. "Mama," I say, "go back in your room. Take Anna with you." Mama does what I say without asking questions. She must be real tired to listen to me so easy.

I go to the kitchen and get the rifle from the corner. The banging grows louder as I tiptoe to the front door. I open it slow and peek out, holding the rifle down by my side. I look up at the two men standing on our porch. Baldwin-Felts detectives.

"Is your Mama home?" the taller man says, scratching his beard and digging in his coat pocket for something.

"Nobody here but me. What you want?" I look at 'em with the deadest eyes I can. I don't give a shit who they think they are.

"We're investigating some reports about your brother Ezra. We'd like to talk to him and your Mama. Either one of them here?" He don't look like he feels any emotions at all. He speaks flatly, the same way he looks at me.

"No, they ain't," I say.

I slam the door and he catches it with his foot. "We've heard some rumors your brother been causin' some trouble. You let him know we stopped by. We'd like to straighten this whole mess out," he adds, then slowly removes his muddy boot from the door. I slam it.

I take a deep breath, walk over to the window. I watch 'em get in their motorcar and drive off. I put the gun back in the corner.

Mama comes out. "I heard," she says. "I reckon they heard about the meetings here but I don't know how. Do you?" She walks to the window. "Katie, when you see your brother, you tell him I ain't allowing no more of that meeting in this house. I believe in the cause, but I got my girls to think of first. Them men ain't to be fooled with."

I follow her into the bedroom.

Anna sits on the edge of the bed. She pouts. "Them Bald-Men-Feltses are mean."

I get back in bed.

Mama sits on the bed next to us. She says, "It's not time to get up yet, Anna. If you wanting to sleep, you can. Katie, I get you up soon to help me take in some washing. We got to start doing other folks washing for some extra getting 'round here. Since the miners been striking they ain't paid but half rent the past month." She kisses me on my cheek and walks out. I watch Mama's feet as she limps out the room, her long dark quilt, and chocolate colored hair swinging behind her.

I begin to feel my eyelids get real heavy and start to close.

FIFTY-ONE

Anna May

I shoot my marble, and it goes rollin' outta bounds on down the alley, bouncin' off a few little rocks. I sure am tired of chasin' these darn things all over the place. I sure wish I could play 'em in the house so they couldn't roll so far.

"Hi Anna." Golden says. He's walkin' over to me. "What you doin'?" He picks up my marble and hands it to me. I don't say nothing. Katie says he ain't no good, so I believe her. "Hey, Anna, you seen Nandi 'round your house much here lately?" he asks.

What he askin' that for? I ain't tellin' him nothin'. Golden's dumb. "Did I tell you 'bout what Ben—the stupid goat—did to Camille's pet pig?"

"No, you sure didn't, but I'd love to hear about it." He chuckles.

"Well, Ben done chased Pig all over the camp, and Pig was goin' SOO-WEE all over the camp! Stupid Ben chased Pig 'round all day long, knockin' over flower pots and stompin' folks' flowers and knocked over Saul's spit can too. That was real nasty. It smells so bad.

"Yeah, they did that and Saul took off after 'em hollerin' 'bout I hate y'all stupids! So then, after they done ran circles 'round and 'round Delphia in their yard, Pig finally got an idea and runned under Camille's house and Delphia was outside hollerin' at it for to get out from under the porch but Pig wouldn't hear none of it! Pig just hides underneath there all day long. And you know what that damned ol' Ben did?"

He looks at me funny. "No, Anna, I don't. But won't you tell me what Jennie's been doin' here lately? She been talkin' to Nandi a heap?"

He asks me more dumb questions. Why I want to talk 'bout that junk? I ain't got no care for who sweet on who. I want to tell my story.

"I tell you what Ben did, the stupid goat. Darn stinker figured out Pig was under that there porch over at Delphia's and he banged his head against the porch all day long like this: BANG! BANG! BANG! BANG! He fell down ever time he done it, too! You could tell it hurt his head, but he so stupid he just keep on doin' it like BANG! He fall down. Get up. Do it again. BANG! He fall down. Get up. Do it again. Over and over. And Pig was smart 'n stayed under there. Pig screamed and squealed real loud SOO-WEE! SOO-WEE! like he was hollerin' y'all help me! Help me, y'all! But nobody helped Pig, 'cause nobody wanted Ben after 'em. Saul wouldn't even get down off the porch. He just swatted a broom at 'em while he hollered. Well, thank goodness, Delphia finally comes out and she goes, What on God's great green earth's goin' on here? Pig, you ain't supposed to be in the yard! I hate you, you gal darn stupid pig! And you too, you gal darn ignorant goat! Camille, get your damn pig back up in the hills like he supposed to be! Get his stinkin' butt out of this yard! And finally the stupid goat, after banging his head against their porch like that—BANG! BANG! BANG!—for a real long time, he finally just fell down with a headache. And right then, when that pig seened he wasn't gettin' up that time, he took off a runnin' through the camp again goin' SOO-WEE! SOO-WEE!

Then he come and runned up onto our porch and in the house on the count a somebody leavin' the door open. And it wasn't me. Then he runned in circles in our kitchen, then jumped right up in Jennie's lap and Jennie goes, Damnation! What's Camille's pig doin' in this house! And the pig went SOO-WEE! And Jennie, she goes You don't belong in here. God, you sure do stink! Don't you know you're a pig, Pig? Just then, Ben run in, and he took after Pig like they wasn't no tomorrow and they tore up everythin' in our house, by God! Stupid Ben rammed his big ol' head into everythin' he could find and broke everythin' that wasn't nailed down! He even ate some of Mama's quiltin' patterns. And Katie, she says Ben gonna be poppin' out rainbows for a week."

Golden looks at me all stupid, laughs and then he pats me on my head. I hate it when he pats my head like I'm little. "You won't tell me 'bout Nandi and Jennie, will you?"

I shake my head no. "You ain't got to pat my head like I'm little. I ain't that little."

FIFTY-TWO

Golden

Katie opens the door. "Oh. It's you," she says. "What you want, Golden?" She rolls her eyes at me.

"I come to see how your mama's doing. I brought y'all some of this bread my sister Tara made. She feels real bad 'bout your mama. She. . . ."

"All right, Golden. You ain't got to beg."

"I told you and told you I was playin' that day, Katie. I'm sorry you got hurt. I never meant for you to. I care about y'all."

"God, you here to ask for our vote this election or you wanna take that dish in the kitchen?"

"Well, no, I wanted to see your mama if she's well enough, and see Jennie, too, if she. . . "

"Come on in. Not that I want you here, but I reckon you got to tolerate a insect or two in every house once in a while," she says. She waves me in, rollin' her eyes and slammin' the door behind me. I stand here a minute. What she want me to do? I'm 'bout scared to move 'til she tells me to. "Mama's asleep. Can't see her now. Give it here." She jerks the bread out my hand, lookin' at me like she thinkin' 'bout slappin' me with it. God, I'd sure like to slap her sometime. "Jennie's out back. Give her a minute."

I take my hat off and put my head down a little bit to keep from gettin' mad at her.

"Stand here," she says, and pushes me into the kitchen.

The front door opens, and here come Jennie with the

hunkie Nandi behind her. She hugs him, and then he picks her up off her feet, squeezin' her. I'm strainin' my ears to hear what they're sayin' to each other. For Christ's sake, I think I could just throw up and fall over dead. I can't stand that Nandi. She kisses him on his cheek, and he kisses her cheek, then he walks out the front door. He don't look at me much, just tips his hat and goes on. "Well, howdy, Golden. What you doing here?" Jennie says. Afternoon light comes in and splashes all over her hair. It looks red in this light instead of dark brown.

Katie stands beside her, arms crossed.

"I just thought I'd see how you was, Jennie. Wanted to see how your mama was doin'. Brought you somethin' my sister Tara fixed for you. If you're busy, I understand. I can come back later on."

"Well, why don't you sit with me on the swing a while?" she says, smilin'.

Katie scrunches up her face.

"Well all right," I say. I smirk back at Katie and follow Jennie outside.

We sit on the swing. She asks how I been.

"I been pretty good. I'm a little worried about y'all over here." I take off my hat, set it in my lap. Lord, I hope I can have five minutes just sittin' here talkin' to her. She never talks to me no more. "I heard about them boys layin' switches on your porch, Jennie. Some of the whites up this holler ain't happy. They don't want no colored or foreigners up here. To make it worse, you got to go courtin' with one of them. So, you got them white folks to worry about and your brother is in the union and runnin' around with folks accused of shootin' mine guards. Them thugs are gonna pay you a visit unless you get the guilty parties away from your family. There's spies everywhere, Jennie. It won't be long until the company knows exactly who's been doin' what. This union ain't never gonna survive. You heard those colored miners got hung, and the company let the white ones go—the union won't never work now with all the miners fightin' among themselves. You need to just move out of here, Jennie. Damn, there's too much goin' on here for a bunch a women to be right smack in the middle of it."

She looks like I'm makin' her feel bad.

"I'm sorry. I'm worried 'bout you is all."

She pulls her shawl up 'round her shoulders. She picks loose thread from her dress. I don't like seein' her so upset. I don't want nothin' to happen to her.

"Jennie, Ezra told me Nandi decided to pull out of the union and go move into Blue Diamond. He's a scab now. You've done been seen kissin' a foreigner but worse: a scab. Do you realize how many people y'all are pissin' off at the same time? Your family's makin' enemies on every side. Pick a side and stay with it."

"Golden, I ain't afraid of the company or whoever laid switches on my porch. I ain't afraid of the union men that hate Nandi or the whites that hate my boarders. I ain't picking a side. Even if Ezra's union, that don't mean I can't still see Nandi."

Before I can say a word, she's back inside and I'm alone on the swing. What am I gonna do? I see Anna watchin' from the window, wavin'.

FIFTY-THREE

Jennie

Anna snores next to me. I listen to the hard rain outside and wonder about Mama, Nandi, Golden. Finally, I fall asleep and dream. Our clothes are soaked. Katie and I walk through creek water. We're hunkered down like we're hiding. Katie grips my hand, and I lead her through the dark. I feel her fingernails graze my palm as her cold hand slips out of mine. I turn and scream without knowing why. She's gone.

"I can't catch you, Katie! I can't catch you if you fall!" I scream.

There are men sitting on the porch of my house. They're expressionless. Two wear hats with wide brims hiding their eyes. Wet beards and muddy boots. Heavy breathing. Long coats. Black suits.

I'm barefoot in a dry cotton gown. I feel afraid the men may be looking at my breasts. I fold my arms to cover them. Put my head down and walk to the foot of the steps. I see my feet are purple in places and covered in little red scratches. Sore.

I hear Mamaw singing a lullaby, but I can't understand the words.

The men have guns across their laps and on their shoulders. The house catches fire, but no one moves. Flames billow from behind the men and lap at corners of the porch. They sit as if it isn't burning. I walk backward and hold my hands out in front of me.

Then I'm suddenly carried by someone with strong

arms. I feel weak or sick.

Is this me? Do I taste the creek dirt? Do I eat it like when my hands are dirty as a girl and I accidentally smudge it on my cornbread after a day of playing in the creek? Is it crunching between my teeth and making my bread taste like summer?

I see my feet. My hair hangs down wet along my face. Covers my eyes. I can't see anything but my feet and my hair so dark and tangled like the woods. The man carries me through tall brush. I can't scream or move. I stare at the sky because my eyes won't close. My eyes will not close, and the clouds are black and gray. The clouds feel like Mama's lap when I was a child. I'm in the rocking chair in her lap. I hear someone say, "She's dead."

But I'm not. I'm being carried. He's tall. I can't lift my head. I can't swallow. I can't move. But I breathe and look into the sky turning blue-black. A few drops of rain fall.

My eyes are blurry. My eyelashes are dripping.

I hear his feet slosh in mud.

The brush scratches against my face. I still can't move. Another man says he shouldn't have killed me.

Mamaw whispers, "All mens is devils."

I begin to suffocate. I want to scream, No! Nothing comes.

"Jennie, wake up! Jennie!" I wake to Katie shaking me. "You're having another bad dream, Jennie." She pets my hair.

I don't say anything. Just drift back off as I watch Anna May rubbing her sleepy eyes and whispering yawns.

FIFTY-FOUR

Katie

"Katie," Jennie says, "I don't think you really ought to go down there right now. Take that food to Mrs. Mendez after them company men's gone. I need you here to help me anyhow. Set that basket down."

I put my coat on, and my gloves. "Oh, no," I say. "This hole in my coat gets bigger all the time. I can't mend gloves as good as you. Will you fix it for me?"

"Don't change the subject, Katie. Take off your coat. Please don't be going over at Mrs. Mendez's right now. You ain't gonna do nothing but get yourself in trouble."

Jennie's always giving warning 'bout something. I know it bothers her about Mr. Mendez getting killed. Bothers all of us. "I'll just be a little while, Jennie. You worry too much. I'll be back and help you pretty soon," I say.

It's a shame they throwing Mrs. Mendez out of her house. Yesterday Ezra come told us the whole story. First, her brother dies in the mines along with fifteen other men, then her husband's killed for inciting men to strike for safer working conditions. They just shot him down like a dog. Not a day after she lay her husband low the company's already throwing her out into the road like a dog.

Jennie sighs and shakes her head. "Well, hurry back. Don't be down there shooting off at the mouth in front of them men. Give her that basket and come on home."

I pick up the basket and straighten its bow. I made this bow myself. Not as pretty as the ones Mamaw May used to make, but almost. I walk out the door and down the alley. So cold today. Looks like it's a few minutes from snowing. It even smells like snow to me. Jennie always says she smells snow coming. I think I'm starting to know what she's talking 'bout, but for years I just thought she was crazy.

As I get closer to Mrs. Mendez's, I see her furniture laying all over the place as the men in suits pack it out. She sits in a rocking chair out on her lawn. She's holding one of her little girls. Has her wrapped up tight in a blue blanket, and she rocks her. She looks terrified. Her other little girl stands next to her, watching the men move about the property like bees around a hive. I walk up and set the basket next to her. "Mrs. Mendez, we put some things together for you," I say.

She keeps rocking, holding tight to her little girl. The older girl looks inside the basket. "*Gracias*, Katie. *Gracias*," Mrs. Mendez says. She seems on the verge of crying, like any minute she'll fall apart.

"Mama wants y'all to come to our house for supper if you like, Mrs. Mendez."

"We stay with sister," she replies.

I see the same Baldwin-Felts detective that tried to throw us out of our house. Mr. Black. "Well," I say, "it sure is nice to see you again, Mr. Black."

He doesn't respond, just looks at me like he's as happy to see me as I am to see him. I start to feel uneasy. Mrs. Mendez looks fed up and tired. I smile at her, and she thanks me again.

"You're welcome, Mrs. Mendez. You're welcome," I

say. As I walk away I notice Mr. Black staring. "Dirty bastards," I mumble. Behind our camp on the hill is Golden Motley's house. Nearby sits a mine boss's. Not a mine owner's—them don't even live in this state's what Ezra says. The homes on the hill are safe from black dust that clouds the air down here in the valley. Their homes don't all look the same like ours, don't have roofs that sag or porches that fall in. Ain't got ceilings that leak when it rains or windows that let in the cold. I bet they're warm inside.

I make it down the alley and up our porch. I look across the alley and see Nandi standing and talking with one of the men in suits. He's moving into the camp. Damn scab. At least he ain't under our roof no more.

When I get back to the house, our teacher, Mrs. Adkins, is at the table with Mama and Jennie. I sit down and get me a plate of food. Some greens, potatoes, beans and cornbread. I don't say nothing. Just listen.

"I believe Jennie would do well in college. She's my best student," Mrs. Adkins says. She's not touching the plate of food in front of her.

"Mrs. Adkins," Mama says, "I don't know how we could pay for no college. We need Jennie here now. I'm sick and we got Anna to take care of."

Jennie just plays with her potatoes. She looks at me.

I smile a little.

Mama says she don't know nothing about college because ain't nobody in our family ever been to no college. Most of our kin don't go to school past ten. Always too much work needs to be done at home. Who has time for school?

"Mama," Jennie says, "Fannie says there's a way to

pay for it. She says. . . ."

"Jennie," Mama interrupts. She sighs. "I got to get back to bed. Mrs. Adkins, I thank you for coming and talking to us, but I just don't know nothing about this. Y'all two can decide what you want. Katie, would you help me?"

Jennie's face is red. She looks upset.

I don't know what to say.

Mrs. Adkins don't seem to know what to say either.

I get up and take Mama's elbow and walk her to her bedroom.

FIFTY-FIVE

Jennie

Anna sleeps next to me, curled under thick quilts in our bed. I pet her hair, running it through my fingers. This always helps her sleep. I'm just about to fall asleep, too, relaxed by the warmth Anna's small body shares against me. It's turning dark out. Lord, I'm noticing the days getting shorter now.

Today's so cold I can't see a reason to step a toe outside the house. Good thing it's Sunday, or I'd have stayed home from school. Of course, Katie stopped going and Anna May's been complaining about not wanting to walk to school in the morning on account a the cold. They never liked school anyhow. I have a mind to stop going, too. Just too cold to walk in the mornings. The weather is mild one day and then finger numbing the next. It's almost Christmas, and the weather feels like it, too. Today, icicles dangle, long and sharp like the roof has teeth or hair made of glass.

Smoke billows from a far-off chimney, lapping the wind like a gray tongue. I know Nandi don't work Sunday. I just about want to walk to the camp and drop in for a visit. Got to find my gloves and scarf for the walk to school in the morning. I almost forgot about it. I slide out from under Anna, trying not to wake her. I start rummaging quietly through the closet.

I don't reckon I know Nandi through and through. I don't know him like I know these gloves. These are the only pair of gloves I ever had, except for a little pair when I was a tiny thing. I slide my hand into the thick blue mitten and back out. I fold them together and lay them on my dresser. I remember Mamaw May making me the gloves and a scarf to go along with it. She had picked out my favorite color—a real dark blue, and it was just a month or so shy of my sixteenth birthday, so I was thinking she was making something for me. I was hoping it was a quilt like the one she made for Mama when Anna May was born. Anna still sleeps with that thing to this day. Every time I visited her, I'd ask to see what she was making, but she'd always come up with some errand for me to run. Then, she gave them to me on my birthday along with a kiss on my cheek, just like I thought she would. I hadn't guessed it'd be mittens, though. I thought for sure it'd be a quilt. But I love these as much as if they were a blanket. I wear them everywhere as soon as it's cold enough outside. They're worn. Got a hole right in the index finger. I keep this hand in my pocket so not to show the hole until I can get time and fix it up.

I don't know Nandi like I know these gloves, but somehow I feel as if I've been carrying some part of him with me my whole life. So many times through the years I should've lost these gloves, but every time, no matter how foolish it was, I'd never leave them behind.

I close my eyes, and I can see that time Katie and me run up to the graveyard hill to try out that sleigh Isaac made us. Somebody got some new dogs, and the dogs come running after us, growling and barking. They were sure some mean animals. On the way home, I dropped my gloves in the snow. Although Katie was in front of me a ways hollering for me to come on, terrified those dogs would get me, I ran back. I pulled them out of the snow with my naked hands and almost didn't get away from them dogs. I just couldn't leave them behind. Then we ran all the way home. We really were scared.

The first time I saw Nandi, I had to look more than once. I couldn't decide if he was just plain strange looking or beautiful. He was some kind of in-between. It wasn't the first time I saw him but the second or third when I started to really like looking at him, wanting to know who he is. I looked at him, and a feeling welled up inside me like a snowstorm rolling in from miles off. It wasn't love, I don't guess, because I don't know if I have any idea what that even is. But the feeling moved through my body like a whirlwind of blistering cold snow. It whispered some kind of secret. It had to be his eyes. I know it was his dark eyes that said something about being human. He watched me with those dark eyes—the only calm, still thing I noticed in the middle of what I was feeling.

I'm going to walk to camp and talk with him. First Golden, then Katie, and now Ezra telling me to stay away from Nandi. They say people are talking, and I'm bound to get myself in trouble. There's people who hate Nandi because he's a foreigner, then there's the union men that hate him because he went back to work in the middle of the strike. It's too late to ignore him now anyway. I already like him. I've liked him for a while now. How can I pretend I don't? And why should I? I don't care what they say.

Anna's sound asleep. Katie's off at a neighbor's, and Mama's in bed. Nobody has to know. I brush my hair and wash my face. Lord, what am I doing? Nandi's gonna think I'm crazy. I stuff the feelings of doubt and fear down somewhere inside me like I would an over-sized blanket into a tiny trunk. I see our willow tree through the frost-glazed window. I sigh. I got this storm here inside that he riled up, and I want him to know, but what words do I use? I can tell he has a storm, too, by how he looks at me longer than he ever does anyone else in a room, the way he talks to me, the things he tells me. Maybe he don't know how I feel at all? But I could be wrong about all of it. Maybe I just imagine the way he stares at me.

I creep down the stairs. The wood whines with each step. I look. No one is around. I walk down the holler and into the camp. I see there's already new folks living in my old house.

Nandi's door's cracked, so I bend over to peek in-side. The door flies open. I gasp. I search for words. I can't think of a single one.

He takes my hand and leads me inside. He puts an arm around me and cradles my cheek. He kisses me— not a quick kiss, but the kind that lasts a while, the kind you can draw out, the kind that never seems enough. He has been thinking how I was sure he did. Golden *does* have a reason to fear him. I'm breathless but full of words, afraid but feeling the fear falling all around me, dying on the floor. He walks, guiding me backward slowly until I'm against the wall. I'm beginning to for-get where I am. He whispers something in his language. What's he saying? "I am wanting to say, to tell you you are beautiful, Jennie." He kisses me again.

FIFTY-SIX

Ezra

I spit, wipe the sweat off my brow with my sleeve and look over at Saul. We sit alone in the union barracks, waiting. We know something's going to happen the moment that train of scabs gets to the mine and they see they ain't no mine left. Bill kicked the one guard more than a few times. I believe they both probably dead now. Maybe nothing will happen tonight, but something *will* happen soon. We wait. Thank God we built this barracks. The miners up in Mingo are living in tent camps—lots of men, women and children with nowhere to go just because they wanted to unionize. It ain't right. For us and for them. That's why we fight.

They got forty miners up in Mingo County in jail. They was a scuffle between guards and union men. The law hung four black miners for beating them guards to death. The three white men that were in on it got put in jail. The charges was dropped later. Now all the unions busting up. Coloreds don't want to unionize with whites. Italians hate the coloreds. I don't know how we gonna get men together now, not with everything that's happened.

"Everybody fighting everybody," Saul says. "I don't know what we're gonna do."

"Saul," I say, "we got to get all the folks together, or this is just gonna keep on how it is. It's gonna be war inside of a war. Not just union against company, but union against union. It's late. I'm gotta get back."

Jennie

I wake to the noise outside. There's a crackling noise and men yelling. I smell smoke. I don't feel Anna or Katie lying next to me. I rise up. "Anna?" I say. "Katie? Anna!" No one answers. I feel like my lungs can't get enough air.

Mama calls to me from the hallway. I rush out to find her there, standing and looking bewildered. She coughs feebly.

I go to her and take her hands in mine. "Mama," I whisper, "What's going on outside? Do you smell the smoke?"

She can't answer me through her coughing.

"I'm going to see," I say.

The yelling gets louder. I hear a gunshot that echoes from mountain to mountain like thunder in the valley. My stomach feels like blood's spurting into it from the bottom, hot and burning. My heart catches fire in the middle of my chest. I feel I could faint. I pull Mama's blanket around her tight and hug her. "Mama, go back to bed. Just go back to bed. I . . . I'll find out what it is."

"Be careful, honey." She kisses my cheek.

I rush to the front door. I step onto the porch, and two hooded men grip me by my arms and hair. The hoods cover their faces. I catch a glimpse of Ezra and more men in robes and hoods in the front yard.

Mr. Hernandez lays in the front yard. He isn't moving, and he's bloody.

I feel thumbs gouged into my throat and a rope burning my wrists as the hooded men tie me hard and quick. Fire swallows the cross in our front yard. Flames claw at it. The grass around its base is scorched black, sizzling. The rest of the yard is white with frost. I fall to my knees, my nightgown revealing them. The wood from the porch splinters into my knees as I fall.

The men pick me up and just hold me. Klansmen are tying Ezra's hands behind him. He stands shirtless and dirty, his eyes shut tight. They hold him up, and he coughs, spits. Blood oozes from a wound on his forehead. I say a prayer. *Our Father who . . . who. . . .*

I hear screaming from men somewhere. I look to the mountains melting into fog, and then there's nothing, no sound. All the hell and chaos is here in this valley.

Saul runs from the back of the house onto the front yard with Klansmen chasing him. With both hands tied and a busted-up face, he struggles, maneuvers around the Klansmen and between them, stumbling, running in circles. He clenches his hands together and swings at the man before him knocking his hood to the ground. The man curses, reaching the hood, and I see him. He looks up at me. I know his oddly long face. His eyes. He scrambles for his hood. Baldwin-Felts! That ain't no Klansman! The others tackle Saul and slip a noose over his head.

I start to scream, and a man punches me in the stomach. No air. I don't scream. I make no sound. My stomach burns and twists inside me. "You sure are pretty," he speaks, an inch from my face, spitting when he talks. I smell tobacco on his breath. I spit in his face and struggle to kick him. He grips me by my hair and forces me to my knees. He slams my face on the porch. He lifts me by my collar and does it again. I can feel, but I can't. I can breathe and can't. I can move but not. My face tingles as if it's turning to ice. I hear the men walk off the porch to somewhere. I see the dirt through the cracks of the porch and Anna, curled in a ball, her tiny hands cupping her ears. "Oh, God," I mutter, tears streaming into my mouth, mixing with blood. "No."

Dust trickles down on her. She looks up at me through one squinted eye. She's shaking and panting, tears glistening on her cheek. Anna can't see this happen to me. I can't lay here and spill blood down through these cracks. I won't. I pull to get the ropes loose. I squeeze as tight as I can, dig my nails in. Sweat runs into the cuts on my wrists, stinging them. I cry out, then try to hold my breath. Try to be quiet. Anna covers her ears and closes her eyes. Please, Anna, don't open them, Little Bird. Keep them closed.

Smoke rises as ash swallows the cross. Wind breathes the dark fumes and ash around me. I flail my legs. A Klansman comes onto the porch. He kicks me. I must ignore the pain. I can't. I just have to move from here, flip myself over. Eyes blurry, I can't see Ezra through tears, smoke, ash. The Klansman kicks me again, and I cry out.

Shotgun booms. The man crashes on top of me, and I can't breathe. I feel his hot blood spreading over my back, seeping through my dress. It makes me sick, his blood touching my skin, but I'm too tired. Blood trickles from my lips between the boards, drips into the dirt just missing Anna by a little.

Black shoes walk in front of me. Katie. She screams wildly, like her anger is ripping her throat as she wails. "You sons a bitches get off this land!"

She pushes the corpse off me and unties my hands. The yard's dirty with ash. The cross has half fallen. Mr. Hernandez lays beside a night rider. Both appear dead. Saul swings from the tree in our yard, his face and body still contorted in pain. Ezra's beside me suddenly. Katie hands him the gun.

"Katie," he says, "I'm gonna need you to run get Jackson down at the union barracks. Need him and a couple men to help me get these bodies. We need a doctor!"

I tell Little Bird to close her eyes. I close mine as Katie tries to lift me.

FIFTY-EIGHT

Jennie

"Lord, it's getting late," I say.

Nandi sits on the swing next to me and we rock a little, watching the stars come out in the black sky. He smiles. I know he ain't thinking about the time from the kind of smile that was.

"Thank you for coming to my house," I say. "Yesterday was a nightmare. I was so scared." He touches the bruised side of my face and I wince.

He's acting different tonight—nervous, odd. He has this look on his face like he's been thinking too much. I pretend I don't notice. I'm sure he sees I'm pretending, but I'm not sure how else to act.

"It don't hurt much. It'll be okay," I say. "Ezra won't be home from the meeting for a while. Nobody minds that you come to see me."

He's afraid to be here, and I don't blame him. If the company finds out he's hanging around with the little sister of a union man, he'll get in big trouble, and if Ezra finds him here we'll both get in trouble. He puts his arm around me. "I am wanting to see you are feeling all right, that you are being safe," he says.

Carefully, he takes the blanket from around me, squeezes me tight to him and wraps it around both of us. This makes me nervous. Everything he does makes me comfortable and nervous at the same time. I try not to show it, but I know I'm showing it. I'm probably shaking like the flame on a candle. I rest my head on his chest. Feel safe around Nandi. He's the only man I ever felt safe around besides my brothers. Feel like can't nothing bother me when he's around. Not even Golden, who keeps walking by our house watching us close. Golden doesn't trust Nandi.

He finally stops doing that. He must've went to the meeting finally. Golden just worried like the rest of us.

I ain't sure why but I could tell when me and Nandi first met that we've been through the same things when we were both children. I knew it before he ever told me about any of the hard times in Budapest. He toiled in the vineyards the way I toiled on the farm and, when he grew up, he had to learn something new to survive. He had to move away from his home. My family did the same thing, moving from our farm to the coal camp, and now from the coal camp to this boarding house.

He got this look in his face that makes me want to touch him. When light hits his face at night, I see something I understand because it's in me, too. I can see who he was when he was a boy when I look in those dark eyes, and this draws me to him. I think if we had been little together we would've been the best of friends. We would've played together and told our secrets to each other. We're so much alike and so different at the same time. He makes fun of my thick southern accent, and I tease him about his broken English. Truth is, I think it's what makes us so drawn to each other: this sameness broke up by a few differences neither of us could control.

"Jennie, you have clothes warm?" he asks. I know he means do I have any clothes warmer than what I'm wearing. I'm so used to how he talks. So used to him I can hear what he wants to say before he says it just by looking at him. I can tell when he wants to laugh at something or when he yearns to tell me something. I can tell when he hurts, too, from those eyes.

"Well," I say, "I got a shirt under this dress, and this coat was Isaac's, so it's pretty big on me, pretty warm."

Katie comes out on the porch. "Jennie, it's too cold out here. Come in the house. Help me with Anna. She won't get in the tub." She gives Nandi a look of disgust but then shakes her head as if to give up. I know it ain't the cold she's worried about. Yesterday made her hate Nandi more, I think. Nobody in my family wants me to hang around a scab. I guess it's stupid of me, but I can't help it. I feel like I need him. Especially now.

"Katie, I'm fine. Go on in. You don't need my help with Anna. Besides, I always got her hanging on me and you always running free. Take your turn and watch Little Bird for me, please?"

Katie pouts and crosses her arms. She sighs. "Fine." She slams the door, making that face she makes when she's irritated with me. Well, she always forgives me, so I'll not worry too much about her right now.

"I am wishing to go for walk. We walk to the big rocks on hill?" Nandi says, pointing behind our house. I know which rocks he means. The three huge boulders almost like a house. You sit on one and build a fire, and right above it's another rock bending over it like God thought it'd make a good roof.

Everybody is off at that big meeting tonight talking about what happened here yesterday, so that's where company thugs'll go to start trouble if they decide to. Katie'll be fine by herself a few minutes. "I want to," I say.

We stand on the porch just looking at each other.

He reaches out and touches my arm, rubs it. Turns his head a little to the side. "We go?" he says. I always tell him he has the prettiest smile I ever seen, but I know he don't believe me. I'd do anything he says. I look down the alley to the left and right. Ain't a soul around. It's as quiet as it gets when it snows. Feels like it might. I can't believe I'm walking up there right now, but he makes me feel safe, so I don't mind. I pull the blanket tighter around me and take his hand. I take the lantern from beside the front door and light it. We start walking behind the house and up the hill until we get to the tram road. Everything around us is swallowed in darkness. It's just us. Orange dances across his face from the lantern. Above us is never-ending trees, tall trees that separate enough so we can see between them and see the sky peeking through their branches. The sky is lit up like a million lightning bugs have fallen asleep and froze in midair. They get brighter and fade, then brighter again, vibrating in the darkness. One snowflake falls slow and lands in his hair, and then another and another. We both look up and start to laugh.

"I think we're gonna have to turn back," I say.

He pulls me close to him a moment and kisses my cheek. His warm breath shows up like smoke in the cold and moves my hair. I shiver. I notice the way his black eyes contrast with the white floating around us. I can feel myself adding that scene to memory, the way you add the most beautiful things you ever seen to a place in your mind that can't be touched by nothing and nobody. And I add this there.

We start back and I watch the snow spit and swirl, glowing in clear night all lit up by that high, pregnant moon. "Nandi," I say, my voice shaking, "let's go to your house."

He looks stunned.

I laugh. I pull his arm tighter around me. "Katie will be okay for a little while. Fannie took Mama to a doctor visiting a neighbor's house. They won't be back a while. Nobody will know. Let's go," I say. "Please?"

Where's this bravery coming from? What has possessed me? I've lost my mind.

FIFTY-NINE

Anna May

I run out back 'cause I wanna see what Jennie and Nandi are doin'. I go 'round the house and peek. I see 'em on the front porch. They laugh and carry on. She act like Katie when she's 'round Nandi. I like Nandi. I'd marry him for sure if I was Jennie, even if Katie don't like him much. Wouldn't want Katie in no wedding of mine nohow. She'd probably get in a fight! I giggle when I see him put his arms 'round Jennie. They start down the steps. I hurry behind the house and under the back porch. Too cold under here. Wet. Hate it. Hope that possum ain't under here right now. They go walkin' up the tram road. I ain't a followin' 'em that far away. "Shoot," I say. "Too cold for that junk."

I see two little green eyes floatin' across from me in the dark. Somethin' hisses. "Fred!" I jump and bang my head on the porch, crawl out fast as I can. "Lord, almost got ate by that gal' darn thing."

I hear men's voices. What's that? I climb up on the porch and peek in through the back door. They's men standin', talkin' to Katie. Who they? They got long coats and hats. Got rifles, too. Oh, no. Katie got her hands on her hips. She puts her finger in that man's face. Looks like she smartin' off to 'em. I close the door back. I jump off the porch and find me a stick. "Get outta there you stinky possum," I say, and throw the stick under the porch. Fred runs out the other side. I crawl under the porch again. I sit here for while.

Them men scare me. Jennie and Nandi will come back soon, and the men might leave then. I'll just stay under here a while and then go see if they's gone.

SIXTY

Katie & The Creek

I know there was a knock at the door. I remember this. But my head hurts so. On one side, it hurts. Something hot runs slow down my eye, into my eye and down my cheek, into my mouth. Tastes like metal. Rust. I'm bleeding. I know these hands carrying me must be taking me to Mama. Strong hands. Like . . . Isaac?

He ain't taking you to Mama, Katie.

Hush.

Who said that? I must be talking to myself. I must be. Because my head hurts. Sounds like me. Did I say that out loud? My insides hurt. I feel swollen. I see my hand hanging down. It's big and red. My fingers are bending the wrong way. My wrist's the wrong way. I'm scratched.

Don't look, Katie girl.

Hush.

I turn my eyes away. I won't look at my fingers again. The trees are moving above me. Move and step and sideways and step and bump and step. It's getting dark.

My head rolls to one side. I see the broken split-rail fence as he steps over it. Lantern. Split-rail fence in the dark. I hear male voices.

"Don't know why. Don't know what in hell got into you. Ain't good for nothin'. Didn't have to go this far. Gonna be trouble. You know them white trash down the Branch are crazy."

Someone tells him to shut up.

Is that Ezra climbing in that tree? Looks like Ezra climbing and Isaac with him up high in that tree. I could laugh. In a minute I'll laugh. Instead I cough a small cough. I choke a little on something wet inside my throat. Did I have a drink of water? They should turn me sideways so I can spit it out. It won't go down. It's warm. No, hot.

All mens is devils, Katie.

Hush.

I may cry. In a minute I'll cry. I feel warm tears stream down my face, touch my lip. I don't feel the left corner of my lip, only the tears touching just under it on my chin. It dribbles down my open mouth. Oh, I wanna move. Mama, they ain't taking me to you, I don't think.

Anna smells like quilts. Quilts in December, smoky from the fireplace. In the summer everything in the dirt alleys smell like wet dog when it rains.

Now I remember. Oh, God. No, I can't remember. It's too much. Stop. Stop! Something spins. Spins too fast. I'm scared. It's my stomach as he trudges up a hill. My stomach, and I vomit. Feels better now. Easier to breathe.

"Damn, Bradley! Jesus, she's still alive. Hurry," a man says.

"No, let's not. Let's take her back. She ain't gonna remember nothin'." He's younger. I think he's Ezra's age. "Let's take her back. Come on, y'all. I won't tell nobody what y'all done. Please." He whimpers. Sniffles.

"Shut up! You did this, now shut up your crying,"

another says.

I hear heavy breathing. It spins again, and I see their faces when I open the door, and he says something about my legs. Yeah, Mamaw, they done hurt me, but I let 'em in. But I did let 'em in. He said something about my legs. I hear him say it in my head: You sure is the prettiest girl Mary's got. I told 'em, Don't want no trouble out of y'all, you hear? I remember. I hollered No! Let go! He pulled me. He pushed me down. I felt one of them tear my dress. The other, the one with the big black eyes, he. . . .

Vomit again. Feel myself shaking hard.

My thighs were wet. One held me. He bent my wrist down. I screamed. I cried down his knuckles when his hand was on my mouth. I cried down his knuckles, and I had tears and snot down my face. I screamed into his open hand. Into nothing. I felt him push into me hard. I ripped. I must have. The younger boy hollered for them to stop. We was just supposed to scare her, he said. He told 'em. He told 'em. But he didn't save me. I looked in his brown eyes while they raped me. I looked in his crying eyes as he put his head down. He couldn't watch.

It's getting black. Dizzy. I can't scream now. Why can't I make words? Just sighs and sounds. Hum in my head. The song Greensleeves, how Jennie hums.

My head hit the floor. Corner of the table into the top of my head. Hit me hard.

She ain't good nohow. Feisty though. That's what he had said. The younger one fled outside. Slammed the door. I heard him crying.

Men have no strength, Katie girl.

Hush.

I bit his hand. I still taste his hand. I taste on the side that I can feel. I stare at the sky because my head's tilted back over his arm now. Mama, you come get me now. I'm shaking so.

She ain't, Katie girl.

Hush.

Who is that talks to me? Mamaw?

I'll push myself into the creek water. Push myself across the water. Then I'll run away. I feel my feet go into the water.

"Push her down in there good. No, idiot, like this."

I feel my legs. My belly sinks into cold. My hair's over my face, or is it water? I look up into dark water-sky. I see them through the water, and I sink. I sink slow under bubbles that sing. Mamaw, they singin'. You sing with them now. To me.

I'm sinking. But now I feel warm again. Oh, I think I'm alive. It's fine. I'll fall asleep now. In Mamaw's arms.

Daddy. Mama. I can't cry down here.

No, Katie girl. I'm not them. It's all right.

It's so cold. But it's just so cold.

Hush.

SIXTY-ONE

Old Man in the Woods

I got to get this here shed moved. Lord, them damn men finds my liquor out here, I'll be up shit creek. My lazy ass good for nothin' son got to get his sorry ass down here an' help me move this whole thing. Lord, have mercy. I'm a gonna end up in jail.

I walk with my cane. It sticks in the mud and old leaves rotten everywhere. It sure is getting dark early. Lord, it must be getting winter time. God, I hate cold. Hate the damn cold. I slip, fall, go slidin' down the hillside. "Shit!" God damn leaves. God damn shoes ain't no good. Damn son, where's he at? I be okay if I jus' let myself slide. I slide on down, but they is rock right there in front of a pond. "Oh, Lord!" I'm a headin' right for it. Both my feet crash into it, and I flip over and land right in the water. I know my shoulder broke. Damn shoulder burnin'. I stand up. Grab my shoulder and rub it. Damn, that hurts. Where's my cane? "Gal' darn cane! Where the hell you . . . ?   Oh, my God."

They is a pale white face looks up at me, half sunk into mud on the bank. Her eyes wide open, and her mouth full of leaves and mud. Her long brown hair soaked and stuck to the side of her face. I can tell she was pretty. Her hand twisted up at her side, and her dress floatin' in the water. Her hands covered in cuts. She ain't wearin' no shoes. Little bloody cuts all turned dark red all over her. Bruises. She was hurt real bad by somebody. Her white legs float just below the water and glow under it all white with death. "Oh, little girl." I bend down. "Oh, no." This Clem's and Mary's girl for sure. Her cheeks thin and lips pucker open, purple and swollen. Her eyes shine and look into the sky at nothin'. She sure don't see nothin'. Looks so young and so good. Who would lay hand on such a baby? Feels like she watchin' me, and I can't stand it. Hurts me to look at her. I can't stand it. I feel I might throw up. "You just a baby. God love her," I say. I take off my heavy, wet coat and look at her face one more time.

I can't hardly remember the words to a prayer. Look like she was callin' somebody the way her mouth lay open. I say a prayer best I can, try to close her eyes with my hand, but they frozen like that. They won't move. I lay my coat over her face.

Move my shoulder a bit. Oh yeah, that sure is hurt. Damn shoulder. There's my cane. Stuck right in the mud. I pick it up and start the hard walk up the hill. I fight through the brush. I can't get back to the camp fast enough. My whole body feel like it frozen. My God, the cold. My boots stick in the mud, and I slide down some again. I see her body still movin' easy in the water. I realize I ain't made it nowheres yet. I keep on climbin'.

"Paw, you need my help?" my son hollers. Finally got here. I'm glad he wasn't here earlier.

"No, no I make it up myself. You stay up there, ya hear! I mean it!"

I look up and see him peekin' down over the hillside. "All right, Paw." I know he gonna see her he keep lookin'.

"I mean it!" I holler and dig my hands in the dirt,

clawin' my way up the mountainside.

SIXTY-TWO

Jennie

I can't do this without Fannie. Thank God she's helping me lay Katie out. This is so hard. I just pretend it isn't Katie. I pretend she's the skin of a rattlesnake in August, shed and left lay, a transparent coil emptied of the life that once squirmed there. I feel like I'm asleep. My eyes are almost blurry. I'm calm. I can be calm. I *will* hold on. I pretend this body's a girl pulled from the water, a girl with no name or story. I know my neighbors would do this for me: wash Katie's body, dress her. But I can't let nobody see my baby sister like this, not with these bruises, cuts. I try not to look at her face. I know my mama needs me. She can't do this. Ezra can't. I got to do it. So, when Fannie comes downstairs, I invite her in the room. We sit next to Katie's body. "We got an old table top and propped it between these here chairs. I reckon it'll hold," I say.

Fannie doesn't speak, just looks at Katie. She doesn't cry. I can tell it's by choice.

Mama's in bed. She can't come in here.

Fannie looks at me like she's scared of me. Why?

Ezra brought Katie's body in, with a couple of his friends helping and placed her as lovingly as he could on this old worn table top. She's still got her clothes on at least. Thank the Good Lord for that. But she's so pale and soft from the water, a little bit swollen, but not too bad. Her legs look so beat up, and her hands. Her wrist's broke. How did this happen?

I rest my head on the table top next to Katie's still,

cold body.

Fannie pats my back and I cry.

"Why did I leave her alone?" I sob.

"Jennie, you should let me do this," Fannie says.

"I wasn't there, and I should've been. Nandi come over, and we went off together. Had I stayed, this'd never happened. Do you hear that? What's that noise?"

Fannie shakes her head.

I feel like a part of me's dead on this table with Katie. What matters now? "I won't go with you, Fannie." I say. "I don't want to go to school. I want to die. I want to die, too!" I sob. Feels like I'm pouring my whole self out of my body, draining out my life the way Katie must've the last time she breathed in the murky creek water. Someone stole her breath the way a cat draws it from a baby sleeping soundly. When Mamaw May told me about cats stealing breath from babies I imagined green-eyed black cats creeping into the creek and slithering their way back to hell where other night terrors go, wherever the creek ends. "How could I have left her!"

Ezra walks in.

"Ezra, it's my fault. I'm sorry! I never imagined something like this could happen if I left for a little while! Just a little while!"

He bends down so he's level with me and pulls me to him. "Don't, Jennie," he says. "Come on, let Fannie do this, please." I hear his voice fill with tears like a barrel ready to burst. I lean into him and cry on his shirt. I feel him begin to cry, too. I ain't known Ezra to cry, not my brother, but he loves Katie, too.

My eyes never sparkled like Katie's. Now her eyes

seem gray as her skin. Her body's strewn with leaves and dirt from the water.

"I'll do it, Jennie. Get up and go with Ezra," Fannie says. "I don't need help. You can go in there and rest." She takes my hands in hers.

"I got to be here!" I holler. I rip my hand away from her. "I got to do this for Mama. I can't just leave Katie. Go on, Ezra. I can do this. Fannie will help me."

He doesn't argue, just gets up and goes.

"What am I gonna do without my sister?" I say. "All that's happened, all this. What am I gonna do?"

I rest my head on the table with Katie's cold body. Then I stand and finally look at Katie's face. If I don't look, I won't be able to stay in this room. "Here, help me cut this dress off her," I say. I feel my voice through my head. My whole body seems to vibrate inside quietly, but I try not to shake. A hum drones in my ears, matching the vibrations in my body. I can't make a sound. There's a hum, like a song in my head, blocking out any noise.

We slit it down both sides with knives careful not to cut her skin. As we peel off the tattered dress, the smell of flesh and the creek permeate the room. I feel as if I may faint. I start washing her up. We wash away the red from the cuts across her breasts and hips, around her mouth. The suds drip from the rag onto her wrist, her shoulders, as I drag it from one part of her body to the next, and the hum . . . the hum drones and drones in my body, my head. Everything looks blurry somehow, like I'm looking at everything through a dirty window. I have to take lots of time to get this grit out from her nails. A couple of them are broke real bad, split clear down to the flesh of her finger. I take the necklace

Mamaw May gave her from her neck carefully, so I can brush her hair. I set the locket next to her. We lift her body. She's very heavy. We start trying to put the new dress we made on her. The drone in my ears. The hum. Hmm. Hmmmmm.

It's almost like there never was life in her to begin with, like she always been this way, like she never could run or talk or fight, like she's broke. "But she ain't broke," I say. "She must not be really, not our Katie girl. She was a force of nature."

Fannie looks at me strangely.

The hum.

She lived like a storm, like the kind that drags blue-gray shadows through the alleys, cooling the searing July day. Now Katie has no colors in her at all.

I fall quiet and stare into space.

Fannie touches my arm. She says something.

The humming. My skin splits. I'm making a fence. My neck's a split rail fence. Split the rails. Split.

I feel something twisting behind my eyes like a worm. I feel my calm slipping from me, a blanket ripped from my body in the morning when I'm cold. The hum. Cold fingernails. Splinters under my fingernails. Hum. My chest begins to hurt. My breath starts to feel cold, like cold fire entering and leaving my mouth. My tongue's numb. The roof of my mouth's frozen. Can you feel that cold? I feel like something's moving down my skin, like something's begin ripped away, like my skin's being pulled off. My stomach shakes like a branch. Shakes. Hums. The room begins to tilt. It looks like it's moving. She looks like she's slipping. No. I can't. The smell! I can't stop breathing so hard. I see Fannie bend down to look at me. My eyes roll up to look at Fannie's face. I'm in the floor. Fannie speaks. I can't hear what she's saying: words, but not words. I crawl to nowhere. I crawl in a circle. My neck's a split rail fence. An axe is peeling at the back of my head. I could vomit. I scream. I look at the knife in my hand.

Fannie grabs at it.

"No, don't!" I scream. I scream until I can't hear myself scream. I hear the ring, the long buzz, the hum in my ears. The hum's slipped out of my ears: a bee's stinger pulled out of my ear. Sound's all sucked into a tunnel.

Fannie tries to grab me, hold me.

I hold the knife tight.

Over Fannie's shoulder I see Katie's leg slip from the table. "Her leg! N-no!" I cry, laugh. I push Fannie from me. I look at the knife. I look at it.

Fannie yells something.

I slash at my leg. I slash my arm. I cry out as blood runs from me, and I smell the smell that makes me want to vomit. The smell's an axe peeling at the back of my head. Split rail fence.

Ezra comes in. I see his feet.

I lay against the floor. I kick at Fannie. I slash at my arm. I want to bite the floor. I just drool.

"Ezra! Help me!" Fannie screams. Her voice comes back now from a tunnel.

Is that me crying? It is. I hear myself crying. My voice comes back from the tunnel. The cuts burn. Blood runs. It's hot. I cry and scream.

Ezra lifts me, carries me out of the room.

I slap at his face. I kick and writhe. I pull my hair

out. I put my hands to my mouth. I taste blood. "Put me down, Ezra. Put me down!" I breathe . . . breathe. My breath slows, and my tears, my stomach, like a rattle . . . a rattle. Rattles out.

SIXTY-THREE

Jennie

Been a week since we buried my sister. I wear long sleeves over my bandages. I won't think about that right now. Haven't had the energy to go anywhere. I want to lay in bed like Mama's been doing, but I can't. I got to do the washing and cleaning. Got to cook for me, Anna, Ezra, the boarders, and Mama, too, even though she doesn't eat no matter how good I fix supper. Mama seems on the edge of dying—more from losing Katie than the consumption. I've never seen Mama this beat down. Just going to take a while is all. I wish I could sleep all day. Wish sometimes I could close my eyes and not wake up. But then I think of Anna, and how she's just a little thing—my Little Bird—and she needs me to whisper secrets to. I'm the closest thing she's got to a mother while Mama's so wore out. If it wasn't for Ms. Garrison and Anna, I believe I'd turn crazy. All I do is cook and clean and obsess about the investigation. I keep asking Golden about it every single day but he never has any answers. He keeps putting me off, saying they're doing the best they can, but I just don't feel like it's good enough.

Fannie should be home soon. She helps me with the washing, and the cooking and cleaning, too. She keeps talking about going back to the college where she was teaching and leaving Caney Branch. She says now that the miners are on strike there's little need for a school for colored children. No one's been going to school since the fighting broke out, and there's no telling when it'll end.

The fighting's changed everything. Ezra's so caught up right now with the union that we hardly even see him anymore. I knocked on Nandi's door earlier, and he never answered. He ain't answered his door in about three or four days. Seems like neither Nandi or Golden any damn where to be found when it matters. When I ain't no good to Golden, ain't making him feel like I'm his puppet on a string, he ain't nowhere. Just comes around smiling when it suits him. Acts like his is the only life really important. And where's Nandi? He's here when nobody's looking, when there's nobody to disapprove of me and him but, in the daylight when folks can see, he acts like he's just a former tenant and I'm only the daughter of the lady that runs the place.

The other day Ezra said he seen Nandi together with Maria Hernandez. If he lays eyes on that girl he won't talk to me any more. I'm sure glad I don't still live next to her. Can't stand watching her. He couldn't be spending time with her, could he? He's working and working, more now that so many miners are on strike. What time's he got to give her? Maria's too much for me to think about, but I see her face everywhere like a ghost. She's like a church with painted glass windows and perfect choirs that sing high and beautiful. She's a church with fancy pews and blood-colored velvet crawling down the center aisle. She's got a slender body and long, tan legs that take her up above anyone like me, or at least that's what Nandi must think if Ezra's telling the truth.

I ain't sure my brother'd lie to me about such a thing, but I know he's scared of how folks'll act if they saw me and Nandi together. Maybe he'd lie about it for my own good. Union would want to kill Ezra if they thought he had anything to do with a scab. Maybe he's telling lies to protect us both. Can't say I blame him.

I hear somebody come in the front door. "Jennie, I sure wish you'd reconsider going to the social with me tonight. I think it'll do you good. I really do," Fannie says. She smiles. I can tell she feels sympathy. She's such a good woman trying to get my mind off all this grief and death.

"Well, why don't you just visit with me some before you go? You can finish telling me about the days when you were back at the university. I sure like your stories."

"Jennie, please come out with me. You need to get out of the house. You'll be glad you came once we get there. I hear they got a band coming. I know you love music."

I sigh and walk to the door, then peer out the window at Anna. She's in the alley playing with Camille and Sam like always. I look at the kids playing and laughing. Anna's strong. She's resilient like a water dog or a dandelion.

"You're so unhappy here, Jennie," Fannie says. "I wish you'd rethink coming away with me and going to college."

I don't want to think about college. I'd rather think about Anna, and how I used to be strong as she is. I sure wish I had her strength or Katie's courage. I take in a deep breath and almost cough from the dirt I riled up sweeping the house earlier. "I don't really want to go to the social tonight, Fannie. But I'll go anyway. Maybe it *will* do me some good. Give me a minute to clean this dirt off my face. I look like a coal miner." I don't feel like being anywhere at all. I almost wish I could disappear between the cracks in the floor like dirt that's been down there for ages. But I can't disappear, so I'll go out and fight this heaviness. I'll fight it without Nandi or Golden. I'll fight it knowing I won't wake up as anybody other than myself tomorrow morning. That just has to do because it's how it is.

Once we arrive at the social, I feel like coming was a better idea than just staying at home. The social's held at the old schoolhouse building. The railroad tracks run behind it. We make our way up the concrete steps and through the double doors. So many people are here. Seems like the whole of Caney Branch has come out to listen to the band, dance, talk to neighbors. I feel a bit shy. I ain't in a mood to dance, but I'm glad to be here.

Anna runs about with Camille. It's good to see her playing and laughing. Sam has separated from them just now and taken up with a group of boys. Everyone seems to be having such a good time you'd hardly know there was any strike going on at all.

The band's a big group. They dance around as they play, and the singer looks like he's about to fall off stage he's so drunk. I never did see the beat. People dance to the music, and men drink and laugh out loud like there ain't a thing wrong in Caney Branch.

Me and Ms. Garrison sit in the back of the room at an old round wooden table with wobbly legs. I look around the crowd and notice someone I didn't expect to see. Nandi's here. He notices me. Should I go over to him? I smile at him and wave. I start to get up, and Fannie gently takes my wrist and pulls me back. "Jennie," she says, "you don't want to go over there, honey."

"Well, why not?" I ask, turning to look at Nandi again.
I see Maria beside him. How had I missed her face?
Oh, no, I looked like a fool waving at him. I feel
embarrassed, though I ain't sure why. I ain't done anything wrong. *He's* the one made me believe he cared for
me. I'm speechless. I plop back down in my seat. He
puts his arm around her. There's not enough air in this
Godforsaken room. "Ezra told me," I say. "I didn't
believe it." I have no idea what to say next. I sit with
my mouth open. I think I'm about to cry, but I won't
because I'm not going to cry in front of him. My God,
he's just like Golden, only I never realized it. All those
times he wasn't around, he said he was just scared to
come too much on account of Ezra being in the union
and not wanting to get him in trouble, but now I know.
How could I have done what I did with him? It meant
nothing to him. I feel something sinking inside me.

"It isn't because he doesn't care for you, Jennie,"
Fannie says. "I'm sure he cares for you. But like Ezra
told you, you two are from two different worlds. Being
with you would take courage Nandi must not have."
She's awful sweet, but I don't think she's right.

I fold my handkerchief over and over, unfold it, fold
it again and again. I feel like people are staring at me. I
know how I must appear to everybody, and I don't care.
Maria looks over at me cautiously with those eyes of
hers. Nandi pretends I'm not even here. He doesn't
even glance my way. That coward, he knows I'm here.
Look at me, Nandi! "He won't even look at me, Fannie.
I'm just not worth all the trouble to him. I guess it's
easier to be with her. Damn him." I turn my eyes away.
I know when I get home later, this'll hurt me. For now,

though, I'm gonna be mad. At least I won't cry.

Golden walks over to me. His eyes are long like heavy rain-soaked sheets hanging on a clothesline. What the hell's he feeling so sorry for? "Jennie, can I -" he starts.

"Get away from me, Golden. You' ain't nothing but a coward, too. Both of you just cowards. I don't want him, and I don't want you either!" I stand and walk away.

Fannie follows and puts an arm around me. We walk out behind the building where we're knee deep in cold grass, and where nobody can see.

I put my face in my hands and cry.

SIXTY-FOUR

Ezra

I walk from the boarding house to Blue Diamond Camp to find Nandi.

Jackson nods his head. "I seen him a few days ago," he says. "That's where's he's been all this time. He's done moved in with that Maria Hernandez. They got married. It's easy to see he's got to be the one who spied, but we ought to wait until a better time to fight with him, not break up a social in front of the whole camp."

Neighbors watch us pass as we head toward the social.

"That hunkie got to be a spy," I say. "Had to be the one to tell 'em who shot them guards. He's the reason Saul and my baby sister are dead."

Golden stands outside the double doors of the old schoolhouse. He grabs me by my shoulders. I push him away and walk into the crowd. People are everywhere, dancing and drinking. A band on a small wood stage plays dancing music. I search the crowd for Nandi's face. Golden follows me. "Ezra," he says, "don't be starting no trouble with Nandi here. C'mon, if you was anybody else I'd have to arrest you for this shit. Now, I help the union as much as I can, but I can't keep getting y'all out a trouble all the damn time. Ezra, please." He tries to grab me again.

I push him out the way. "This ain't got nothing to do with you, Golden. Go on home if you want."

"Now, I'm the goddamn sheriff, and this got plenty

to do with me!"

He ain't gonna arrest me.

My sister comes up to me with Fannie Garrison. "Ezra," Jennie says, "What's going on? What're you doing here?"

Nandi sits at a table with Maria Hernandez.

I walk toward him.

He stands. He knows what's about to happen. "Ezra, I . . . ," he starts.

I shove him to the ground. "Get up, you son of a bitch!" I holler.

Golden tries to break up the crowd gathering 'round us.

Nandi gets up and backs away.

I want to kill him. I don't know how to stop myself. How can I stop myself? My brother dies in the mine. My Daddy dies in the mine. My best friend's hanged. My sister died ugly. My other sister cut herself half to death. I want to take my hands and put 'em 'round his neck like somebody did my baby sister's, and I want to twist the life from him. I grab a piece of wood from beside the coal stove in the middle of the room.

Ladies scream. People scatter.

I swing. He ducks, and I miss. He runs for me and grabs me 'round my waist. We both fall to the ground into a long row of chairs. We roll. I pin him down with my knees, and I throw my fist against his face. My knuckles scrape on his teeth. I hit him again, and blood flows. Ain't no telling whose it is. Golden tugs at my shoulders, but I don't quit. I hit Nandi again and again. Golden pulls hard, and I fall back. Nandi lays there.

"Let's go, Ezra. Let's just go," Golden says, pulling at

my arm.

Nandi sits up, catching blood dripping in his palm.
Jennie stands next to Golden. I hear her faint weeping.
My head swims. I look down at my hand and see blood.
Mine or his, I ain't sure. "Feels like I broke it."

"Jennie, y'all get outta here," Golden says, just loud
enough so I can hear. "I'm takin' Ezra to the union
barracks. They're having a march tomorrow. I'll be
back later on to keep an eye on y'all while he's gone"

I don't look at Jennie. I don't look at anyone.

SIXTY-FIVE

Nandor

Dearest Janos,

You can no share this letter with family. I have terrible mistake I have made. A girl has died because of me being there with her sister. I was not knowing the men who sent me meant for me to cause this thing that has happened. This death. The men were saying to me they only want to be looking around, not hurt the young girl. They lied to me. Now she has died. Now war has broke out as well. Janos, there is much hardship and suffering here.

I will be moving at once to the place called Illinois or maybe to Virginia. There are places to work in steel mills and also coal mines.

Tell my dearest family only this. I have young wife now named Maria. I will write you when we are reaching our destination and I will be sending money as soon as I can send. I love you Janos. Say all the prayers for me.

Nandi

SIXTY-SIX

Anna May

"Camille, come into my house with me!" I holler.
Camille stands in the alley. "I can't, Anna. I gotta go
home! My mama made supper, and I sure is hungry!"
She runs off.

Well, I just go in by myself. I knock the snow off my
boots a little and run in. Slam door. Oh, almost forgot
to kick off my boots. I kick 'em. "Hey, Jennie! Me and
Camille, we built a snowman, and her dog done ran
straight. . . ." Who's that cryin'? I hear somebody cryin'.
"Jennie?" I say. I go 'round into the kitchen. Jennie in
the floor on her knees. Look like she kissing the floor
all bent over like that. Fannie's at the table. "Jennie?" I
say. "Why you cryin' for?"

Jennie got her face covered with her hands. She gets
up, sits in the chair and bends over, holdin' her stomach
like she might be hurtin'. What's wrong? Why's she
cryin'?

"Jennie?" I say. I run up to her. I grab her hand and
shake it. "What's the matter, Jennie? Ms. Garrison,
what's the matter?"

Ms. Garrison rubs Jennie's head. She look at me and
don't say nothin'.

Jennie just keep right on cryin', that cryin' you can't
help but cry. Like when you sick or somethin' else real
bad.

Ezra looks like somethin' upset him, too. I start to
run into the bedroom to see if Mama's in there, and Ezra stops me.

"Let me go! I wanna see. Where's Mama?" Now I cry, too. I fight with Ezra for him to let me go. I get away from him and run into the bedroom to see. "Mama?" I say, walkin' over to the bed where she layin'. "Mama?"

She don't move. She just lay there asleep.

I get closer. I touch her hand. She's cold. "Mama, wake up."

Mama's eyes closed. Mama's hand cold. I feel the other one. Want to make sure it ain't just somethin' wrong with this hand. It's cold, too.

"Little Bird . . . ," Jennie says. I turn 'round, and she squat in the doorway, reachin' out for me to come over to her.

I hold onto my Mama's hand. I squeeze it hard. Still she ain't moved none. "I want my mama! Make her wake up, Jennie! Make her wake up!" I run to Jennie.

She scoops me up in her arms and hugs me real hard to her. She starts to cry again, and I feel her tears come through my shirt.

I start to cry, too. "Mama come back. Mama have to come back."

"She ain't gonna be able to come back, Anna. I know she wants to. She loves you very much. You remember that. I ain't gonna let you go. I'll hold onto you," Jennie says.

I hide my face in her hair. "I want my mama!" My face hurts 'cause it scrunches up and turns and feels stuck when I cry.

"Jennie, get her out of there," Ezra says.

Jennie carries me to the kitchen and sits down with me.

I cry and cry, and it don't take no trying. It just comes out.

Fannie touches my hair. She bends down and puts her arms 'round me and Jennie both.

It feels hot in here. It's snowin' outside, but it's real hot in here now. My face is hot.

My eyes hurt. My throat feels like it got somethin' stuck in the middle of it. I want to go to sleep. I suck my thumb and close my eyes.

Jennie quits cryin' so much and rocks me.

SIXTY-SEVEN

Jennie

I sit in the family room staring at the wood in our floor. Anna sits on my lap, her arms draped around me and her face in my hair. I can't look at Mama's body. I can't look at anyone in this room, just the floor, the window, my hands. I sigh deep.

Anna whimpers.

"Hold onto me, Anna. Just hold onto me," I say quietly. I rock a little, and this reminds me of when Mama rocked me when I was a girl, how she rocked Anna. I hum the same hum she did.

I ain't got a daddy or a mama. Nowhere's home now. I just stare at Mama's pine box, careful not to see her face. Family's all around me. The house's plum full. Fannie Garrison sits next to me, with Ezra on my other side.

"You want to see her before they close it?" Fannie asks.

I feel something sink from my chest and into the pit of my stomach. I can't make words. I just shake my head no.

Anna cries, tiredly. "Jennie . . . sleepy."

I stand and turn quickly so I don't have to see them nailing the lid shut on Mama. I can't feel all this just now. It's too much. I'm angry, but at who? I missed her leaving because I went to a social. My sister might be here if I'd stayed that night. I ain't thought of nobody but myself.

"You don't have to look, child," Fannie says, patting my hand and putting an arm around me.

Golden walks over.

"I ain't goin' with 'em to bury her if you don't, Jennie. I'll stay here with you."

I say nothing, just cradle Anna close to me and feel the warm tears rolling down and down like rain. I go quietly to the bedroom. I hadn't realized Anna fell asleep.

"She's so tired," Golden says, putting his arm around me after I lay Anna in bed. He hugs me for a long while, and we just stand there.

It's snowing. As if God knows. I hurt so much, and I've cried so long I made it snow. It's as if something in me grabbed the clouds in heaven and pulled them open so snow could float down. I stand near the window and wish the snow would cover my eyes a while. Outside, nothing's black with coal dust. White mutes the landscape.

"Jennie," Golden whispers, motioning for me to come out of the bedroom.

I do, but I stand there, facing him with my arms crossed, and I say nothing. I'm not amused with him.

"Jennie, I don't know what to say, but if there's anything you need, just ask." He has this look in his eyes like he might cry. What's this? He cries? Golden Motley actually can cry? It's like pearls on a pig, or something ridiculous like that.

"I didn't care for nobody but myself," he says. "I was stupid. It took me seeing you with Nandi, to make me realize. I mean, not only Nandi. I seen you with him, and then I seen you in all this trouble, and I realize I care for you. I feel real bad for how I treated you before. I shouldn't have cared what nobody else thought. I didn't. Not really, I mean . . ." He wraps his arms around me. He must be so sure I'll cry in his arms.

This makes me want to slap him. For once, I believe what he says, but it don't matter a damn bit. Maybe there was a day when he still had time to comfort me. I push him away. He stands there, mouth gaping   in shock. He shakes his head almost like I *did* slap him. "I wanted . . . no, I needed your comfort many a time. All these years, Golden. Now you finally got all the comfort in the world? You don't care for me. You never did."

He steps back, struggles for what to say. "Jennie, get that fool outta your head. If he cared for you he'd be here when your mama died. But is he? I might not a been here for you before, but I'm here now."

"Golden, why's everything always a chance for you to prove yourself? It's always about you, isn't it? Loving me, not loving me—it was never about me at all, was it? It was about you and what whoever you loved or didn't love said about you and your goddamn fancy friends and family! To hell with you. You don't know who you love no more than you know who you are. But I ain't mad. It's all just waste. Sheer waste. And you've always had everything. You'll never understand the meaning of the word 'love' or 'waste' or anything else, and I ain't got no more time to teach you."

Mama always hates when you waste anything. I feel the same way. And I feel how she must've when she'd hold up the family in bad times. I feel like I can stand here without nobody and nothing to hold me up.

I wish Golden would just hush. Why's he still talking? What's he even saying? Something else about how he cares for me, about how he's sorry he didn't realize how badly he treated me. "You never so much as sen me when you looked at me. You still don't! Now, that just ain't good enough. *You* ain't good enough."

He looks at me, confused. He starts to say something else, then sighs and stands there. Finally, after a long silence, he walks away.

I breathe out like I been holding my breath a while. I walk into the bedroom and sit on the bed next to Anna. She's asleep. I wrap a quilt around me and walk over to the window. A bird chirps, laughing, as it bounces onto a skinny, snowy branch. Wind blows. Snow glides in the dark evening that sparkles in blues and grays. "You're both cowards," I say to no one.

SIXTY-EIGHT

Jennie

I pace in front of the window. All day I been packing our things, wondering where me and Anna will have
to live now that all hell broke lose in Logan County.
Been worried sick. Ezra's been in the fighting. The
neighbors tell me what news they get. "Oh, Fannie," I
say, "it's just been the worst stories I've heard, just the
worst. I wish Ezra'd get home."

Fannie sits at my kitchen table and rocks Anna May.

The door. Who's at the door? Oh, please God don't
let it be trouble. I take the rifle with me, and walk to the
door. Anna follows after me. Before I touch it, the
door opens, and Ezra walks in, dirty and looking like he
ain't slept in a week. "Ezra!" I scream, jumping to take
him in my arms. Anna grabs his leg and squeezes. I
feel tears welling up in my eyes. I can't believe he's all
right. "Thank God you're home," I say.

"Lordy, Lordy," Anna says. "You sure does stink,
Ezra!"

He laughs, sets his rifle in the corner, then peels Anna off his leg. He picks her up. "Oh, I missed you, too,
Little Bird. "I sure am glad to be home. Is everything
packed, Jennie? We got to get out of this house as soon
as we can. We'll go stay with Uncle Cletis. Nobody'll`
find us there. There's gonna be lots of arresting going
on here soon, and I'm probably gonna be one of 'em,
I'm proud to say." He hurriedly takes off his coat. "I

ain't sure what's gonna happen now. We'll come back after it's settled down."

"Everything's ready to go, Ezra," I say. "I knew you'd want to go to Uncle Cletis's. I heard Mother Jones is gonna speak to the miners in Charleston. Do you think it's safe enough to go? I'd like to hear her."

He wipes his face with his sleeve and sighs. "Damn women," he says, laughing. "Y'all are crazy, you know that?"

I reach out to hug him. "Oh, please, Ezra? Please?"

Fannie folds her arms and smiles. Anna hangs from my dress. I shift my weight so she doesn't knock me down. We stand silently.

"No, it isn't safe. We need to get out of here quick."

"Whose mama is Mother Jones, Jennie?" Anna asks.

"Mother Jones," Fannie answers, "is the strongest voice the United Mine Workers of America has. She is every miner's mother, yes."

L e a v e s

I dangle in the cool air, nestled in the bough of a silver maple tree. A squirrel climbs near her trunk and sits on a limb observing what I too see, the moon, looking pale and sick, crowned with a ghost-like silver shadow. The stars shiver in the same freezing wind that cuts through the branches and severs away a few of the last leaves left clinging to my tree. Suddenly, I'm shivering. I too float gently and I'm spinning in the wind and I hear myself crackle while a piece of me is torn away. I come down and spin in a tunnel of wind. Fi- nally, after a slow descent I begin to see lights, dozens of camp fires, lanterns, and people sit around drab tents.

I fall close to one of the fires and scream for a moment then a breeze lifts me up again and I land on a child's coat just behind his ear. The boy sits at the campfire and cries to his father, "Why can't I march too, Daddy?"

I can see fear and doubt glistening in the father's eyes and for a moment the child seems to notice it too. The breeze picks me up again and twirls me over onto a tent. There's a mother with long brown hair wrapped in a shawl, her breath clouding in the air as she sings to her baby in the cold.

A man in dirty overalls approaches and kisses her forehead. I twist up into the wind again and it carries me easily in her hands up into the night air, up and up spinning in the cold where now I see all the dozens and dozens of campfires and lantern lights like hundreds of tiny eyes ablaze. A single flake of snow falls. I tremble.

SEVENTY

Jennie

I put my coat on and go outside to sit on the swing. Anna and Fannie follow. The camp seems to be a ghost town now. The trees look like hands of a skeleton, bony fingers all entangled. The dead fingers seem to be reaching, stretching into the sky as if they'd just love to pull it down and wrap its colors around them. Maybe because there's hardly no life left down here. "The mountains look sad with no leaves, don't they, Anna?" I say. "Do you think they're sad?"

"Yep, I think they might be." She nods. "It's too cold out here for me, Jennie." Anna hops down and goes in the house.

"What am I going to do now?" I say, still studying the joint-like knots and splits in the tall tree that bends over the dead grass in our yard. "I ain't got a Mama. I ain't a wife or mother. So, who am I, then?" I hesitate. It's the funniest thing. I hate these mountains, and I love them, too. "At least if I stay here, I can say I'm part of this land. I can say this is the place my family's from. I don't know how I'd feel living somewhere without hills. But I can fight for what Mother Jones fights for, for what Ezra fights for." Feels like the only thing I am is these hills. And these trees.

Fannie grins and pulls out a tattered blue book from her handbag. She thumbs through it carefully. Each page is scribbled on like a journal. "Jennie, I'm leaving tomorrow," she says. "I'm going back to the university to take up my old teaching position. I wish you'd reconsider coming with me. Anna would get a chance at a good life. Ezra could find work. And you'd make a wonderful student, and a teacher later on." She smiles.

I sigh. I don't know what to say.

She stops on a page with a leaf in it. "Ah, here it is," she says. She takes the   leaf from between the pages. It's flat and thin—so thin you can look through it. I do. I look through it, and it covers the world in red-brown spider webs. "I want to give this to you. Take it everywhere you go. This will remind you that, no matter where you are, mountains or no mountains, there will be leaves. What you are doesn't stay here if you do leave and what you are will thrive here if you do stay. Just remember, no matter what you do, you'll   do   well. Don't be afraid." She pats my back the way Mama used to, then stands up, tucking her book under her arm.

"Fannie, thank you," I say.

I touch the leaf, looking carefully at the tiny line that runs up the center and fans out into more lines, all connected like wrinkles on a face. I think Fannie's right. I can't stay here because I'm afraid. But I can't leave because I'm afraid. What do I want? What's left? There's nothing for me here. I have to go with her. I'll suffocate if I stay. "Fannie, I want to be a student. Will you take us with you?"

She claps her hands together.

"Wonderful!" she says.

I think about Golden and Nandi. I think of my family, those living and dead. No loss seems to matter. "I never felt like I was much good to anybody, Fannie. I want to go somewhere else and, I don't know, just try to be good for something."

SEVENTY-ONE

Anna May

"Bet you didn't think I was out here, did you, Jennie!" I say, laughin'. I crawl out from under the porch.

"Anna, you silly thing. How did you get under that porch! I thought you went back inside," Jennie says. She's laughin', too. Jennie comes out of the alley back onto the yard. She picks me up. "Oh, Anna, you're coal black. It's so dirty under there! Let's get inside. We're going on a long, long trip tomorrow . . . to a city. And I'm gonna go to a great big school, Anna. I'll teach you everything I learn when you get old enough." She hugs me hard and laughs, bouncin' me on her hip.

"Hey Jennie, what you figure she wants you to do with that leaf? You figure if we plant it, it might grow a whole slew of trees with leaves that very same color?" I take the leaf from her. It's pretty.

"I don't think so, Little Bird. But you can plant it anywhere you like. Let's go tell Ezra where we're going. Think he'll come with us?"

I laugh, and Jennie runs with me on her hip into the house.

SEVENTY-TWO

Jennie

I wear the only hat I own: my Mama's gray Sunday hat. I look out the train car window through the gray netting of my hat and rub my hands together, feeling the soft insides of Mama's gloves on my fingers. Anna and I sit on one side of the train car, and Fannie sits on the other. Anna stands in the seat waving out the window at Ezra who blows kisses to us from the terminal.

"He'll come for us later, won't he, Jennie?" Anna asks, whimpering, kissing the glass and waving frantically.

"I imagine he will," I say.

"Ezra can't stay gone from you two for long," Fannie says, smiling.

I watch my brother sling his hat back and forth as we pull away, and I see Jackson pat him on his back as he appears to wipe a tear from his face. I breathe in deep and shake some when I breathe out. I feel a sting of longing for Ezra already, and for Mama, my sister, my Daddy, Mamaw and, a little bit, even Nandi and Golden.

Anna lays her head in my lap and begins sucking her thumb. I pull a blanket up to cover her legs and rub her back in circles.

Somehow for the first time in my life, I feel like my heart's full. Full of both joy and sorrow, sure. But it is full, and no one filled it for me. It just is. I can't wait to see what's on the other side of these mountains. I've never been so sure of anything in my life.

Tears push behind my eyes, but a smile comes, too, all on its own. I pet Anna's hair as flecks of snow swirl in gusts past our window.

Anna sucks her thumb and begins to hum "Greensleeves."

Epilogue

Snow

I sit, a drop of mist on the edge of a cloud, then I slip through as it gently breaks, falling into a steel-colored sky. The smell of wet ground and rotting leaves rise from the trees below. A parked passenger-train parts the dead mountains for miles and miles. I descend slowly, falling from the grey sky as a drop of round, soft water. Then, bone crack cold wind spins me in her hands. She rocks me, cradling me in her palms, lulls me, kisses me goodnight with icy lips. I feel myself change. Inside, I crackle—a bright pop! I disappear for a moment, then return as thin, webbed ice. I've become snow, wearing a delicate costume like small feathers of a dove. Now, wind sifts through me, softly. Growing outward, I sway slowly down the mountainside, zigzag through the valley. A small crowd of snowflakes dance nearby.

The windows of the train cars below glow and pulse with light like hearts. Behind them, shadows of mothers with babies in arm hum songs that seep from window cracks.

Suddenly, hundreds of me burst into the night seemingly from nowhere. I descend in a whirl of thousands of other snowflakes as passengers below board the train, snow landing on their hats and in their hair, melting on their gloves.

A man stands by the train, waving outside a passenger window, "I love you! Take care of Jennie, Little Bird! Take care! I miss y'all both already!!" I swirl around his wrist as he swings his hat to wave goodbye.

Children crowd in the windows straining their necks to see their cousins, friends, and aunts waving their goodbyes. Darkness descends quickly, finally drowning the last bit of sunlight as if in black water.

The other snowflakes sing or say something about the past. The smooth black sky punctuated by clouds blinks stars. I approach my own end toward the black train's wheel. I am unafraid. I'll return to the ground and return to the clouds again.

"We'll see you soon, Ezra! We'll see you real soon!" the woman holding the little girl says, waving as I land on the cold steel, slipping down the groove.

Men die in winter and in the spring babies are born and all the death is forgotten again for a little while.

ABOUT THE AUTHOR

Andréa Fekete is granddaughter to Mexican and Hungarian immigrant coal miners. She was raised in Riley coal camp in Buffalo Creek, West Virginia. She has one poetry chapbook, *Dear Lovely* (2020). Her poetry & fiction appear in many journals & anthologies such as *Chiron Review, Borderlands: Texas Poetry Review, The Kentucky Review, The Montucky Review, GoldenSeal Magazine, The Adirondack Review, ABZ,* and in anthologies such as *Eyes Glowing at the Edge of the Woods: Fiction & Poetry from West Virginia,* among others. She & Lara Lillibridge co-curated *Feminine Rising: Voices of Power & Invisibility* (2019) an anthology of 70 award-winning & emerging women writers from around the globe. The book took the Silver in Foreword Review's Indie Book of the Year in Women's Studies. An excerpt from her unpublished novel *Native Trees* was a finalist in *Still: The Journal's* 2019 Fiction contest. Fore more about the author, visit hollergirl.com.